Never Far
International Bestselling Author
in Erotic Horror
A.A. Dark

Never Far

International Best Seller
in Erotic Horror
A.A. Dark
Copyright © 2017 by A.A. Dark

ISBN: 9781521416228

All Rights Reserved

All characters and events in this book are fictitious. Any resemblance to persons living or dead is strictly coincidental. The scanning, uploading and distribution of this book via the Internet or any other means without the permission of the publisher is illegal, and is punishable by law. Please purchase only authorized electronic editions, and do not participate in or encourage the electronic piracy of copyrighted materials. Your support of the author's rights is appreciated.

Prologue
Lucy

Some people have life figured out. Fear doesn't hold them back. They chase adventure and live their days to the fullest. They don't calculate what could go wrong or let things like addictions control their every move. They have passion. Maybe it's toward their job, or as small as making the most out of their day—food, hikes, seeing that certain someone smile over the smallest gesture made on their behalf.

Love.

I was ruled by love. I wish I could start this story with an unforgettable meeting of how boy meets girl. With an instant connection leading to a romantic confession of undying love and devotion. But that's not how life or love works. Not for me. Not for Boston Marks.

It was February. Cold, gloomy—devoid of any real color that would uplift one from the winter blues that swallowed almost all northeasterners whole. I was supposed to be at work serving refreshments at our local rundown theater when I decided spying on my brother, Jeff, and his best friend, Boston, would be more entertaining.

They were camped out in the backyard. Boston held a fancy video recorder to his eye, his dark brown hair falling over his other, while Jeff was covered in fake blood, wielding an axe over his head as he yelled toward the lens like his life depended on it. For the independent film they were making, it did.

For weeks, I sat in the shadows, watching, wishing they'd ask me if I wanted to star in their movie. Once, Boston had started to mention something about it, but Jeff warned me to back off. From my earliest memories, he couldn't stand me being close. I liked to think it was because of our age difference, but I knew better. He and Boston were in their early twenties, and I was fresh out of high school. Since my parents split up and I took my dad's side, the verbal and physical abuse had only gotten worse. Boston, on the other hand, threw me looks I could only assume were bred from pity. It was the most I could get out of him. He had always been quiet, hiding his thoughts, staring at me but never getting close. For years this continued, and for years, I held to the hope that he'd feel something for me too.

"Stay away! Stay the fuck away from me or I'll kill you!"

Boston moved in closer, bending his knees and lowering just the smallest amount as the axe swung within a foot of the camera. Sweat dampened Jeff's hair despite the biting chill in the air, and crimson and dirt smeared his face. I hugged around my chest, burying my chin deeper in my jacket as I leaned against the side of the house.

"I'm serious, man. Get the fuck back. You're crazy!"

Mumbling something I couldn't hear, Boston rose, moving the top of his body to the side as Jeff swung the axe eerily closer to the camera. My pulse spiked, and despite knowing I'd get into trouble if Jeff found out I'd skipped work, fear led me into the open.

"That's it. Feel it. I'm going put this down—" Boston ducked, jerking the lens up as the axe split the air just above his head. I gasped as my brother wielded the sharp edge back toward his best friend. Maybe it was my presence, or maybe Boston had heard me, but his face snapped in my direction and a cry tore from my throat as the blade embedded just above his temple with a loud thunk. Blood ran in a crimson river, flowing over his eye as the camera fell from his grasp. Jeff was frozen. I was screaming while the love of my life stared at me. And Boston...a smile tugged at his lips as his knees buckled before he fell.

Chapter 1
Boston

Angel. I had seen one—or someone I thought was one. She had been right before me. Somewhere. Blonde hair. Green eyes. *Flawless*. A real angel? No…a girl. There was a girl, and now she was gone, transitioning from female to male. *A man*. A man yelling at a woman with dark hair. They were young. Mid-twenties. His jet-black hair was slicked to his scalp. Biker. Tattoos. A large hand lifted and blood flew from the side of her mouth in slow motion, the connection causing me to slow in front of the rundown bar.

City. Lights. The hum of traffic.

Strobing colors brightened and faded as a light glow suddenly surrounded me. Wooden walls. A cabin. Metallic perfume burning into my nostrils as large brown eyes looked up, pleading. Disgust rolled through me, and I smashed my fist into his face once again. Rage over what I had seen left me unhinged. *Blonde hair. Angel*. Her young face flashed, then an older boy who looked strikingly like her followed. Abusing, hitting my girl. *Mine*.

The faint memory barely wormed through, but somehow fed the heat encouraging my hand to slam into the biker's face with more force. Flesh split under my power, oozing red. Flowing like a river of death—a death that would find him soon enough. I knew this place—this me.

Blonde. Blonde.

The scene wavered, but rushed back as I brought my knife up. The man's eyes rolled under swollen, lacerated lids. The need to embed my blade through each one was there, but that wasn't where he had hit the dark-haired girl. No.

"P-Please."

The mumbling brought a smile to my face. I licked my lips, flattening the metal against his chin.

"*You like to hit women?*"

His mouth opened, bringing his bottom lip level with the point of my knife. Before he could speak, I pinched the thick meat and drove through the center. The pop from the layers of skin turned to resistance while I sawed through muscle toward his cheek in one direction, then moved back to the middle of his lip to slice toward the other cheek. Deep screams echoed from the walls as I ripped through what remained. The chunk of lip jiggled in my fingers while I brought it up so he could see.

Exposed, bloody bottom teeth open and closed as he screamed from pain—yelled *for help*. Help. Help. No…he'd find no help here.

Collection. Movie. Tape. Recording. Happiness.

****

Beep.
Beep.
Beep.

"What did I tell you about coming here, Lucy? *Go home.*"

Beep.
Beep.
Beep.

Another man. *An older man.* Eyelids. A chunk of cheek.

A black abyss.

****

Beep.
Beep.
Beep.

"You missed work again?" *Whack!* "What did I tell you?" *Whack!*

"Jeff, stop. You're *hurting* me!"

"I'm going to hurt you a lot more if I find you here again. I told you to stay away. Boston is crazy. He did this to himself."

"You did this! I hate you!"

Shuffling.

"Get off me! You're not my—"

"What? Your boss? Out, now! I better never catch you here again."

A sob. A slam of the door. A second of silence.

Beep.

The void—a breath of time.

****

"Hey, Boston. It's me again. I say that every time I come. *So stupid*," she mumbled. "It's me, Lucy. I know you probably can't hear me, and I'm sorry it's been a few weeks since I've visited. Jeff would kill me if he knew…I'm so sorry I distracted you. I feel horrible. *I miss you so much.* It's not the same without you. I want you to get better. I want you to come back."

Pressure squeezed into my hand, though I wasn't sure how I knew. I didn't physically feel the touch, but something within the darkness told me this person held on tight. Heat sparked in my core. Urges combusted, twisting, igniting. *Awakening*. My heart made itself known—*thump, thump*. One set of beats. Two. Gone. A weird heaviness pulled me back under, seductively smothering me, whispering lustful, violent-filled lullabies. Energy detonated from within the pitch-black oblivion and rage festered stronger than before.

Beep.
Beep.
Gone.

Exposed bone from the bridge of a nose.

A flap of skin wiggling between my fingers.
My yells. Anger. My fist as a meat tenderizer.
BAM!
BAM!
BAM!

****

Light flickered, blinding me. My eyes squeezed shut, and a woman's voice registered. Tingling prickled the bottom of my foot and my leg jerked at the strong sensation.

"Yes, he'll be awake again soon. I'll get the doctor."

Confusion had instinct bringing my lids up again and water pooled at the brightness. Someone was hovering above me. Brown haloed her head as her blurry figure leaned in closer.

"Boston, it's Mom. Oh, Boston, we've all been praying so hard for you. Honey, can you hear me?"

She sniffled, and I tried to turn away, but I could barely move. My legs and arms felt weak. Stiffness had my entire body aching as I managed to shift the tiniest amount.

"It's okay. You've been coming in and out of it for two days. Do you remember anything?"

A moan left me, and I flexed my jaw, making another sound. It was easier than the first.

"Shhh. It's okay. The doctor is on his way. It's so good to have you back. You have no idea how worried we've been."

Lies. All lies.

I wasn't sure how I knew, but my gut told me I was cautious of this woman who called herself my mother. Recollection was absent. Did I even know her? Irritation flared. She wasn't who I wanted to see. Who that person might have been, I wasn't quite sure. There was a girl. A blonde-haired girl. I knew her. *I wanted her.*

Sleep beckoned, and I gave myself over to it. There wasn't intrigue to figure out answers. In truth, questions didn't even come. I felt nothing. Cared about nothing. Familiarity accompanied the realization. The girl. She was the only thing making itself known. She was with me—in my mind. Maybe even inside me. I wasn't sure how that was possible, but we were meant to be together. Fog took over my mind and I told myself I'd think more about it later—after I slept. After this woman was gone.

How much time had passed, I wasn't sure. My eyes flew open at a deep voice. I wasn't as out of it as I'd been before. Three faces stared at me—the dark-haired woman, a gray-haired woman, and a tall, slender man with red hair. He paused, flipping through his chart, eyeing me. It was only then I noticed another man way off in the corner. He was older too, mid-fifties, and powerfully built under his suit. His white hair and dark eyes triggered something, but it faded just as fast.

"Boston." The dark-haired woman came back to the bed. *Mother.* Yes, hadn't she said she was my mom? "Welcome back, honey."

"W-Who…? I cleared my throat, barely able to swallow at the dryness. Water was quickly poured, and my head was lifted. I sucked from the plastic straw, eyeing the redheaded man wearily as he came around to the other side.

"What's…" seconds went by before I had the strength to continue, "happening?"

"You were in an accident, honey." The woman glanced from me to the doctor, but came back to me. "Poor Jeff was devastated. He thought he killed you." She paused. "Well, he sort of did, but they saved you."

It took me a moment. The name bounced around the emptiness and I shook my head. "Who's Jeff? Who are you?"

"Me?" Fear drew in her features and her gaze shot to the red-haired man, her eyes pleading. *Doctor.*

"Amnesia is fairly common considering the circumstances. Boston, can you look ahead for me?"

I wanted to tell him I already fucking was, but light blinded one side, then quickly jumped to the other. He put the tiny flashlight back in his pocket and wrote something down on a clipboard. As he did, my agitation grew.

"Can you tell me your name—first, middle, and last?"

"Boston," I managed. More searching. More blanks.

"It's okay. No rush. Do you know where you are?"

"A hospital?"

"Yes. Good. Do you know what town we're in?" Nothing. "It's okay. Don't push. Can you tell me anything you might remember? Anything at all."

"Uh..." More time passed as I tried to gather my strength. "There's a girl. Blonde hair. I can't remember what her face looks like."

The woman beside me shifted, looking to the white-haired man in the corner.

"All right. Anything else?"

I yawned, exhaustion creeping back in. Flickering scenery had the hospital room fading. A small, rundown cabin wavered into view. One of the windows was cracked in the far left corner, and the door hung open, leaning off-balance from the broken hinge at the bottom. I was in a forest. Trees towered above—bare, dead. It was cold as I spun in a circle. Blood covered my hands. So much blood. Looking down, my shirt was saturated in it. And I was smiling...*and running*? No, not merely running, I was chasing after someone.

"I'm Boston Marks. No middle name." The words flooded from my mouth, but I had no idea where they came from. I was staring at the doctor, only just seeing him as the vivid pictures vanished from my view.

"Perfect. That's all for now. Why don't you get some rest?" The doctor motioned with his head to my mother, and the nurse checked some things on a computer screen before following all three of them out. I closed my eyes, seeing dark. Seeing my salvation. I liked this place. I didn't want to be awake anymore. If I returned to nothingness, I could have her back. I could keep the blonde and do whatever I wanted. And there were so many things. *What*, exactly, didn't come—just a desperate need buried in my subconscious I couldn't decipher.

Minutes went by, and my door sounded. I refused to open my eyes or give anyone else my attention. Not that I really had a choice. As much as I wanted to fade away, my newly awakened state didn't allow me to. I hung between the curse of awareness and brink of unconsciousness.

Footsteps approached. Light, barely existent.

"Boston?"

My mind fought through sleep despite the soft, feminine voice.

"I won't stay long. I came to check on you. Your mom said you're awake. That…well, that you woke up and have amnesia. I'm so sorry." I drifted at her silence, only to jolt awake as she continued. "I'm not sure I can come back for a few days. Jeff will be keeping a close eye on me once he finds out your back." She paused. "I should really go. I just wanted to—"

"*Wait.*"

Chapter 2
Lucy

For over two months, Boston had been in a coma. To see his once muscular frame pale and lean made me sad. The guilt I carried over what had happened had no limit. Endless weeks of nightmares plagued me. Sometimes, I stayed hidden beside the house. Other times, history repeated itself. My screams sounded the same as that day: horror-stricken; terror-filled. They constantly drove me to his room. I read to him. Sang to him—it didn't matter that I couldn't carry a tune. Sometimes guilt made us do things we wouldn't normally have the courage to do. When you loved someone, what was humility compared to blame?

"*Wait.*"

Boston's forehead drew in, pulling at the dark red scar running from just above his temple down past his ear. The once long hair that had given him a bad-boy appearance was now shaved short against his head.

I stepped forward, not sure whether he was awake or talking in his sleep. He'd spoken before while still comatose. They said it was normal, but I hadn't thought so at the time. Moments went by before he finally opened his eyes. When he did, I froze. My heart jumped, then soared. The man peering up at me didn't resemble the Boston I had known my entire life—which was ridiculous since it had only been two months, but it was somehow true. He was a stranger. Older and more appealing, despite his haggard appearance.

Hazel eyes blinked, and his fingers twitched before he managed to reach out to me. My brother's confession came back.

"*You don't know what I do, Lucy. He's done things. He wanted to kill me to hide the truth.*"

"Is that how you're justifying what you've done? It was my fault, Jeff. I distracted you both. Boston's not crazy. I saw what happened. I heard the two of you making the movie."

An aggravated sound was all he had given as he stormed from the room. I was left with nothing but questions and a fear my brother wasn't holding up as well as he portrayed...which wasn't well at all. Now, he was drinking heavily and didn't come home sometimes.

"You."

Boston tried to clear his throat. His gaze went to the table next to his bed, leading me to follow. Grabbing the water, I lifted it so he could get a drink. The pressure he applied to my fingers as I tried to break away gave me pause. It was obvious he didn't want to let me go, but the action was so unlike him. He'd always kept his distance.

Slowly, he sipped, staring at me the entire time. The moment I put the Styrofoam cup down, his arm shakily inched in my direction.

"I know you."

Cupping his hands in both of mine, I nodded. Butterflies fluttered in my stomach, and I smiled.

"Lucy," I offered.

"Lucy." A weak smile. "That's right. Lucy...Little Lucy."

My brow drew in. *Little Lucy.* Was that a good name or bad? Boston had never referred to me in that way. At least...not to my face. Perhaps he thought of me like I assumed he always had—a little sister.

"If I'm bothering you, I can leave. I know you were sleeping. I just wanted to check on you before work."

"You've come before."

"I have, but how do you know that? They said you just woke up."

His head went back and forth and a ragged breath shook his chest. "I don't know. You'll come back. Tomorrow? No...later."

My lips parted, surprise rendering me speechless.

"You will...won't you, Lucy?"

"I'll try. I'm not supposed to be here."

Seconds passed. "Says who? Jeff?"

I gave a nod. "What happened between the two of you? Jeff...he says you've done something. Have you?"

Silence.

"You can tell me if you did. I won't tell a soul." His eyes narrowed as he stared deep into mine. "Boston?"

"I can't remember. Truthfully, I don't know who Jeff is. But you...*I know you.*"

Again, butterflies. My heart swelled, and I held his fingers tighter. With each blink, it appeared tougher for him to stay awake.

"I should go."

"Stay."

"I can't. I wish I could, but if I miss work, Jeff will know. That won't be good. I'll try to come back soon."

"Today?"

Dread increased, but I nodded. "Tonight. I'll try to come after they think I'm asleep."

Lifting his arm, Boston brought my hand to his face. His nose moved along my index finger, and my breath caught as his lips pressed against it. The action was sweet. Intimate. It did something to the woman in me—the one I hadn't known existed before this very moment.

"Keep your word, Lucy. I'll be waiting..."

His eyes closed, and I eased my hand free before spinning for the door. My adrenaline was at an all-time high and I wasn't sure what to do. Should I really sneak out of my house and attempt to slip into his room in the middle of the night? What if I got caught by Jeff or one of the nurses? There were visiting hours, and I wasn't one to break the rules. Well...aside from anything concerning Boston. He had always been my exception.

The door opened at my pull and I nearly collided with a large man with white hair. Apologies rushed from my lips, pausing whatever conversation he was having with Mrs. Marks.

"Lucy. How was he? Did he speak to you?"

"He did." My smile wavered as the kiss came back. Tingling raced over my body, but I pushed it away as I stared between her and the older stranger. "He said he remembers me."

"Did he go into detail on how he did?"

My gaze darted toward the man, locking on his dark brown eyes. The man was staring at me so hard, it made me uncomfortable. "No. Just that he did. He wants me to come back later. I..." My eyes snapped to Mrs. Marks. "I'll try, but Jeff won't like it."

"Don't worry," she said, grabbing my hand. "I won't tell him you were here. I know he's taking things really hard."

"Yes. I...I don't understand it, but maybe now that Boston is awake he'll get better. I should go," I said, removing my hand and stepping back. "I'm already late for work."

Without another word, I waved, taking off at nearly a jog. The halls were relatively empty as I made the turn and headed toward the elevator. When I finally got to the double doors, I rushed through and grabbed my bike from the rack. The mile to the theater didn't take me long. The smell of popcorn greeted me from the main area and I waved at Sarah, my manager, as I headed to the break room. I barely had my purse in my locker before a voice caused me to jump.

"Did I read the schedule wrong again? What are you doing here?"

My hand shot to my heart as I twisted toward him. "Jesus, Greg, you scared me."

"I noticed that. Are you okay?"

"Yes." I laughed, pushing the guilt away while pulling my purse back out. "I'm pretty sure I'm working."

Greg swept his fingers through his oily, curly brown hair. His shirt was half tucked, half hanging out on the side. He wasn't much older than me, and puberty hadn't been kind.

"Nope. See, I'm on today."

I lifted the folded paper so he could look, but there wasn't relief as he scanned over the schedule.

"I'm already here. If you want to take the day off, I could use the extra money. It's cool if you want to get the hours in, I just thought…"

Red tinted his cheek. We'd had this conversation before. Like me, Greg also came from a single parent home, but his mother wasn't just raising him. She had another five kids to support. Greg's income was vital for their household.

"Actually, there was some stuff I needed to take care of. If Sarah says it's okay, I'll gladly let you have my shift."

"That would be great. Thank you, Lucy,"

"No problem."

I threw him a smile as our manager walked in.

"You're late."

"I know," I cringed. "Sarah, is it okay if Greg takes over for me? I ran into Boston's mother on my way here. She said he's awake. I need to let Jeff know."

"Boston Marks is awake?"

At her surprise, I nodded. "Yes. He has amnesia, but I think he's going to be okay. Jeff would really want to know. Maybe it'll help."

There was no reason for an explanation. Sarah and my brother had dated before the accident. Shortly after, he had broken it off with her. We all knew how hard he was taking it and there was a sense of eagerness as Sarah nodded. "I'm sure he's going to be relieved. Tell him I said hello. If he needs anything, I'm a phone call away."

"I'll let him know."

I waved as I hurried out. The truth was, I did need to tell my brother. If he found out I knew before him, there was going to be trouble. And he would find out. When you lived in a town where everyone knew each other, news spread like wildfire.

    A group of kids piled in through the main doors, and I groaned as I glanced out to see darkening clouds. Scooting through the crowd, yells of excitement echoed around the large space, and I sighed in relief as I made it outside.

More cars were pulling in and droplets splashed against my cheeks as I took my bike out of the rack and started home. Like always, Boston stole my complete focus. I let how tonight would work play out in my head until I was easing to a stop in my driveway. My brother's old red truck was parked at a slight angle, crowding the space. The frown was immediate. It told me he was probably drunk again.

I dropped the bike in the grass, and music grew in volume as I neared the front of the house. My mom wouldn't be home. She worked evenings at the diner, which meant Jeff had free reign to get as angry as he wanted. It had me easing through the door. To barge in would put him on edge. Since the accident, any quick movements left him jumpy and short-tempered.

    "What the hell are you doing here? I thought you had to work."

    A bowl of pretzels rested in his lap as he sat on the sofa. Dropping my purse on the coffee table, I plopped down next to him. He popped my hand as I reached over to grab a handful.

    "I asked you a question. You get fired or something?"

    "Sarah wouldn't fire me. You know that." A sadness showed, but faded just as fast. "Greg asked to take over my shift. You know how they need the money."

    "We need the money."

    I paused. "Yes, but there was something I needed to tell you. It was more important than being there."

    "Yeah? What?"

I stood, turned down the music, and took a seat on the far cushion. Distance was key. Distance gave me time if I needed it.

"I ran into Mrs. Marks on my way to work."

"So?"

Jeff tried to hold in his anger, but I could hear the difference in his tone.

"Boston's awake. He came out of the coma."

Pretzels fell from Jeff's fingers, and what felt like an eternity passed as he stared ahead in a daze. I expected yelling, maybe some sort of explosive reaction. Nothing. Nothing but what looked like fear.

"Jeff?"

"Yeah?"

"What did you mean about Boston before? I mean…what happened? I don't understand."

A river of brown poured from the side of the bowl as he slid the pretzels down. Jeff leaned his forearms on his knees and bowed his head.

More time.

"Jeff?"

"Start packing, Lucy."

"W-What?"

"*Start packing!*"

I flew from the sofa at his outburst, shaking my head as I back-stepped toward the door. "Why would I pack? Jeff, you're scaring me."

"You're afraid of me? Lucy, it's not me you should fear."

"Then tell me! What happened, dammit. You treat me like a kid, but I'm not a little girl anymore."

A roar tore from my brother as he stood and started pacing. Continuous sounds left him before a sob took their place. I froze. My brother never cried. Ever.

"We killed a girl, Luce. We fucking killed her."

The wall stopped my retreat and blood rushed over my tongue as my jaw clamped shut. Fear tightened my throat as my brother cried harder.

"It was for the movie. Boston said she would make a great Polly. And I agreed. I mean, when he showed up with her, I thought, what the hell? Sure, why not. We went to this cabin. I didn't even know Boston had a cabin! He was my best friend. I've known him since grade school and I had no idea. There was this stuff. These...*devices*. Fucking handcuffs and shit. Weird shit. Anyway, we were all drinking, and the next thing I know, Boston picks up this sort of...fuck, what was it? Like one of those old fashion irons. The heavy ones. Cast iron, or something. Anyway, he grabs it and just slams it into the side of her head. Blood goes everywhere. She hits the ground—out cold. And I'm yelling at him, freaking out, as he drags her to the bedroom. God, Lucy. Fuck. I should have left. I should have gotten the police. H-Hours. *Hours!*"

Glass shattered as Jeff gripped the pretzel bowl and launched it into the wall. I was crying. I knew I was, but I could barely hear myself over my pulse. All I saw was his fear. And my brother was the inducer of fear. For him to be afraid, it scared me.

"He cut up her unconscious body. Then...then, he turned the knife around on me." More soul-deep sobs. "We beat the hell out of her! I didn't want to. I swear I didn't. But it wasn't enough. He made me rape that girl, Luce! I raped her because I was too afraid to react the way I should have.

"But I didn't know," he rushed out. "I didn't know him at all. He's a monster. I thought I saw it in the cabin, but it was only when he said he was going to get more beer that I truly saw. I tried to get her free. I tried to help her escape, but he didn't really leave. He just parked farther down...*testing me*. Playing with me like a toy.

"I carried her for a good half-mile before he finally stepped around some trees in front of us. God. *D-Dear God.* It was just a game to him. He loved it. You should have seen him. He knew I was terrified, but he…he…fuck. J-Jesus. He's going to come back and kill me. He's going to kill us all."

"No," I breathed out. "No, we'll go to the cops. We'll—"

"The cops! We can't go to the cops! Did you miss the part where I said he made me do this? *Me*. Dammit. Have you not been listening? You haven't even heard the rest of the story."

My hands shot up as Jeff stalked in my direction, his fist cocked back. Just before he reached me, he drew his arm in with a strangled whimper and began pacing. He almost looked afraid to hit me, and he'd never been before.

"You can be so stupid sometimes, Luce. We're not going to the cops. Not me. Not you!"

"No." My head shook as he continued flexing his fist. "Tell me the rest. What happened after that?"

Jeff rolled his eyes, eating up the floor with his sharp strides. "I tried to fight him. He threw a knife at me and told me to end it. I thought I could overpower him—kill him before he made me kill her. I could barely hold the knife by the time he got done with me. I don't know how many times he kicked. I slit the girl's throat and ran home. That's when you found us. He came back for me. He…*Rhonda*. Her name was Rhonda."

"Rhonda?" Something clicked, but I couldn't put my finger on it. Fuzzy thoughts. Then, like a burst of black and white, it came. I pushed from the wall, nausea burning my throat at the vision of the missing girl poster hanging in the break room at the theater. I didn't know her personally. She was two years older, but I'd seen her before. Still, something wasn't right. Hadn't I heard something about her recently? "Jeff, let's look into this. Let's try to find out more on Rhonda. We could—"

"Leave! There's nothing to look into. He's going to come back and kill me, Lucy. He might even try to kill you and Mom. We have to go."

"No, we don't. At least…not yet. Boston doesn't remember anything. Mrs. Marks told me he has amnesia. He doesn't even remember his own mom."

"Lies," he breathed out. "He's lying!"

"You hit him in the head with an axe. He's been in a coma. I think it's possible he has amnesia. You almost killed him."

"I wish I would have. *I wish he was dead.*"

Chapter 3
Boston

She didn't come. Not that night. Not the next day. Not when I got moved to a different room. Time ticked on—slow, torturous. There was an urgency within me I couldn't shake. It ate at me, feeding the mysterious fury within. I found myself snapping at the nurses and anyone who got too close. Even Joy, my mother, neglected stopping by for the last two days, seeming to get the hint.

I wanted Lucy back. I wanted her here so I could see her. The fact that she wasn't drove me to a brink of insanity I couldn't deal with. *Hate.* It was streaming through what should have been a positive time for me. I was alive. It was encouraging to the alternative. But was life really worth living if she wasn't in it? The question raged a battle within. It seemed unfathomable, and contemplation didn't help. There was no debate. Lucy *needed* to be with me. She *needed* to be at my side where I could see her. Hadn't I always kept her close? Watching? Wanting her? Never far from her side?

My damaged mind told me I had. If she wasn't so important, why was she the only person I remembered? The only face I could recall? Sure, scenes of blurry images came—violent dreams of torturing men—but they were irrelevant compared to her significance.

"Dammit!"

I reached over, grabbing the landline receiver. The intense emotions heightened as I stared at the phone, confused over what to do. How the phone worked was common knowledge, but when it came to her number or last name…nothing.

The slam echoed through the room as I hung up, and my finger immediately went to the call button.

"Yes?"

"I need help."

"Is there a problem, Mr. Marks?"

"Yeah. Send someone."

I put the phone back on the end table and turned to stand at the window. Over the last few weeks while in therapy, I learned to walk again. It might not have been very far—I sure as hell wasn't going to be running a marathon anytime soon—but I was getting better. Stronger.

"Mr. Marks?"

A young nurse walked in and visions of...someone blinded me. Teeth broke under a punch. My punch? The colors were flickering so fast. The tip of a knife cut into a woman's chest and the pressure of her skin splitting registered in my hand. I dragged the dull blade, seeing the blood and smearing it over her breast as I turned to smile at someone. The resistance against the multiple layers of skin vibrated my digits as I started again. My muscles were flexing and straining through the cutting.

"Mr. Marks?"

I blinked in quick succession. The vision wasn't right. It had always been men. Never women. *I protected women.* Or...I felt I did.

Sweat covered my skin and pain throbbed in my head. "I need a phone number. I can't remember what it is."

"I'm sorry?"

"A phone number," I snapped. "Amnesia, remember? I need Lucy's phone number."

"Who's Lucy?"

"Jesus, woman, I don't know. Lucy. Blonde-haired Lucy. Young. *Lucy.* Her brother is Jeff. Lucy. Lucy! I need her fucking phone number."

"Calm down, son. It's pointless." My mother walked in, waving the scared nurse out. Her voice was stern, yet soft, but I didn't miss her underlying fear.

"What the hell do you mean pointless? Where's Lucy? How do I get ahold of her?"

"Is she so important to you?"

I breathed through the desire to surge forward and jerk her up so she'd see how serious I was. Being separated from Lucy wasn't working. I couldn't do this. Not a day more. Not an hour more. Not even a fucking second.

"Yes. *She is*. The most important thing in the world to me. I want to see her. I need to speak with her. What's Lucy's last name? What's her number?"

"And so it continues." The words were barely a murmur. She shook her head in disbelief, rubbing her fingers over her eyes. "Like I said, it's pointless. They don't have a phone."

"What do you mean? Why wouldn't they have a phone?"

"My guess is money. They don't have a lot. Boston, we need to talk about Lucy."

"What about her?"

"I think it's probably not a good idea to contact her. Jeff doesn't want Lucy around you. I think something bad happened, and it had nothing to do with the accident. Have you remembered anything else?"

"No." Shrugging my shoulders, I eased back over to the edge of the bed. "Truthfully, Mom, I don't give a shit about Jeff or what happened between us. I want Lucy. You have to go get her."

A laugh of astonishment sounded, and still, I fought that urge to drive in my point. Why was she not understanding? Why was no one seeing how much I needed her?

"Boston, Lucy always comes around. I bet she's busy. If that's the case, we should probably leave her alone."

"You tell me that one more time…" My teeth ground together and I closed my eyes to calm the edgy sensation. "Listen to me. Listen good. *I. Need. Her. Here.*"

Hesitation followed her stiffening. My brain wasn't focusing. I couldn't cope, and I didn't understand why. The only thing I knew was if she wasn't close to me soon, I'd butcher anyone who got in my way of finding her.

"All right. Fine." Defeat showed as she glared at the floor. "I guess I could swing by her house on my way home."

"Thank you." Like water to fire, calmness rolled through. "How much longer do I have to stay here? I'm ready to go home. I'm fine."

Putting her purse down, my mother sat in the chair by the wall. I blinked repeatedly, searching through my memories. "Wait...where do I live?"

"Your things are in the guest house. With your condition, I was able to break your lease. You wanted to move out of that old apartment anyway. I thought it was a good opportunity."

"Right. Good. Tell me about Lucy. What is she like? How old is she? Are we together?"

Another laugh from my mother—one that almost sounded...sad. "Oh, honey." She straightened in the chair. "No, you're not together. She's barely eighteen. I think you wanted to wait until you felt she was ready."

"She's ready. How old am I?"

A pause. More fear? "Twenty-four next month." Her hand rose, flattening for me to slow while it slightly bounced. She was silent. Almost beyond words. "I have to be honest with you. This is the most open you've been with me about Lucy, so I'm trying to adjust. I knew, but...*you're different now*. You used to talk to someone about this—about her. You met him a few weeks ago when you first woke up. Dr. Patron. He had white hair. Do you remember him?"

"Yeah, but not who he is." The last part was mumbled, the realization that my behavior was off eliciting the urge to rein in the overwhelming thoughts. I shouldn't be talking. Deep inside, instinct told me that.

"Boston, are you okay?"

"Am I so different than before?"

She nodded, her features drawing in. "Like night and day. You speak your mind now. You say what you're thinking. You've never done that before. Had you not had a major breakdown at twelve, I may have never even known about Lucy."

"Breakdown? What are you talking about?"

Her lips pursed. "You were a quiet child. Very watchful of everything. I'm pretty quiet, so I always just assumed you took after me. When you were twelve, your dad said you had to stop spending so much time at Jeff's house. You were never home. We hardly ever got to see you. We were worried. Even when we brought you home, you'd run away, back to their house. When you were twelve, you...pulled a knife on your father while we were sleeping. You threatened his life. Even cut him while you had the blade to his throat. You said you couldn't leave her. *Her.* Not him, as in Jeff. We found Dr. Patron after that."

My eyes widened, but it didn't surprise me. I knew what was inside, even if I didn't understand it. "Mom, I do need to see Lucy. I have to. It's...I can't explain it. You just have to get her. I'm begging you."

"I'll go by on my way home. Maybe I'll even talk to Jeff. I would really like the two of you to patch things up. I don't like this tension. I feel like something happened. Something very bad."

Dread. Slight trembling. She was afraid of me...or what I was capable of.

"Well, nothing happened. Jeff...he hasn't been right for some time. I can't...remember, but...he's not okay. He's not good."

"No, he's not. I've always known that."

"Tell me more about Lucy."

A deep breath left Joy. "Later. I'm not sure how much more of this I can take right now. Let's talk about something else. What about school? I'm assuming you'll be taking your last semester off?"

"School?"

"You attend classes at Northeastern. Media and Screen Studies. Does any of that ring a bell?"

"Screen. Films. I make movies." Colors swirled, coming together as an axe swung toward me. I was holding a camera, moving with the flow so I could avoid the blade. A man my age with dirty blond hair…he was angry. *Yelling.* Blood. He was covered in blood. Memories of the men hit hard. "That's right," I said lowly. "I make films."

Pieces came together. All the blood. All the chaos that manifested in my mind. The camera set up in the corner of the cabin's bedroom as I removed chunks of skin. *Movies.*

"I'm assuming you're going to wait, right?"

There was no thought required. "I'm not leaving. I'm staying here with Lucy."

"Boston…" My mother rung her hands in her lap. "You have to realize Lucy has free will. She has a choice. What if she doesn't want what you do? You have to face that, because although you may feel strongly for her, she may not feel the same way. If she doesn't—"

Denial had my head shaking. "No. She's the only one I can remember. There has be something. I…*love her.* And she loves me. She has to."

"She may not. Especially if you've never told her. I don't mean to make you upset, son. I worry for you. But I want you to be prepared. Nothing may ever happen between you."

Rage shot through me for reasons I couldn't understand. The need to attack was there, but I held firm to the urge. "*She loves me.* Lucy loves me. She fucking loves me, and I love her, and that's the end of it."

Silence.

"All right. Maybe she does. Maybe you're right. You're very upset, so we're done talking about it. You're having a hard time with not remembering anything, and I should give you some space. I'll go by and ask Lucy to come see you."

"Thank you."

"You're welcome." Standing, my mother put her purse strap back over her shoulder. As she turned to leave, I felt myself wanting to follow. Desperation was edging back in. What if Lucy didn't come? What if…what if she wouldn't see me? What if she didn't love me like I loved her? No. She did. But what if she didn't come? I needed alternatives—other ways to get ahold of her if this failed.

"What's her last name?"

My mother stopped at the door, glancing over her shoulder. "Adams. Lucy Adams." With that, she closed the barrier behind her. The knowledge surged through me like I'd won some sort of prize. I had her name, and she could never hide. She could never disappear without me being able to track her down. How did I know these things, yet not know anything about myself? There were so many questions, but ones I didn't care to decipher. My mind had only a single concern, and it wasn't for myself.

Chapter 4
Lucy

We were having dinner when a knock sounded on the door. My brother, my mom, and I looked up from the rickety table we sat around, and my mom moved to stand, but Jeff put up his hand and rose.

Confused, I shrugged to my mom as we watched Jeff head through the living room. We never had company. If we did, it was usually because Jeff was drunk and passed out somewhere. We'd gotten three of those visits from neighbors in the last two weeks.

Jeff didn't take well to us not leaving. My mother wouldn't budge in her decision without an explanation, and Jeff wouldn't elaborate past needing a fresh start. I kept waiting for him to disappear and try to take me with him—not that I would leave after what I found. I even tried to convince him, but my brother wasn't well. His story wasn't even plausible. The poster was old. Rhonda...she wasn't missing or dead. She'd ran off with her boyfriend and was now back in town, knocked up. That's what I had forgotten and re-discovered through my search. Nothing he said made sense, and now I didn't know what to believe.

"Hello, Jeff."

"Mrs. Marks. What are you doing here?" My brother shifted nervously, pulling the door more closed around him.

"I need to speak with you. It's about Boston."

"Actually, we're eating dinner. Can we do this some other time?"

"I'm sorry, but I'm afraid not. This won't take long. I just wanted to know what happened between the two of you. This couldn't be about the accident. Or, is it? We all saw the video of the movie you boys were making. It was clearly an accident. It's just...I don't understand why you haven't gone to see him after everything you've been through together.

You're best friends. Was there something else? Maybe before he got hurt?"

"I don't want to talk about it."

"But Boston needs you, Jeff. He's not doing very well."

I stood, easing toward the door.

"He doesn't need me, Mrs. Marks. I'm sure he'll be fine."

"I'm not so sure." She paused, and I moved closer. "He keeps asking for Lucy. That's why I'm here. He made me promise to tell her to come see him. Because of the amnesia, I'm hoping he's confused. That maybe it's you he wants. You boys grew up together." Another bout of silence, followed by her shaky voice. "Jeff, you have to keep Lucy here. You have to go to my son and fix whatever it is that's gone wrong between the two of you. It has to be you."

Jeff's head shook, but he sighed. "I'll try to go by and see him tomorrow. I have to work, but I'll swing by the hospital on my way home. As for Lucy…you don't have to worry. She knows better than to go back."

"Excellent. He's been moved to room two-twenty-one."

Jeff nodded, closing the door. The moment he turned and spotted me, he jolted to a stop. The look he threw was threatening, and I felt guilty for what I knew I had to do. If Boston wanted to see me, I was going.

"Sit down, Luce. Let's finish dinner."

"What did Mrs. Marks say? That was her, right?"

Jeff and I took our seats, and he gave my mom a grin. "She just wanted me to visit Boston. Apparently he's not doing so well adjusting to amnesia."

"Oh, honey, that's horrible. I really do think you should."

Jeff dug the fork into his potatoes, agreeing with a hard nod. He stayed quiet as he kept eating, but I didn't miss the way he kept taking glances at me. My appetite wavered, and I picked at my food as I thought over the last few weeks.

What if Boston hadn't done anything wrong? What if Jeff was the one with a problem? After all, he claimed he killed a girl who wasn't even dead.

Dinner went by in a silent clanking of utensils. Jeff made an excuse like he did every night and disappeared. My mother wasn't much different. She was exhausted from working a double the day before and said she was going to catch up on sleep. I found myself impatient as my need to see Boston grew overwhelming. Before I could stop myself, I was on my bike, peddling as fast as I could for the hospital. Maybe memories returned concerning Jeff. If they had, perhaps he could make sense of what was happening.

Or maybe I was making excuses for what I knew I wanted—*him*.

The hospital was relatively empty except for an occasional nurse. I kept my head down as I walked quickly through his hall. When I found the room and knocked, his deep voice echoed through, and I eased in. Boston was sitting at the bottom of the bed. He wasn't wearing a hospital gown like I expected. He had on a pair of black sweatpants and a white t-shirt. At seeing me, he sat straighter. There was no smile. No expression at all. Just a widening of his eyes as he scooted more toward the edge.

"You never came back."

Anger. It laced his words, but wasn't prominent. Walking forward, I contemplated how close I should go. Jeff's confession had my mind spinning. Even though it obviously wasn't true, I was hesitant.

"I'm sorry. It's not easy coming with Jeff watching my every move. He's even been taking me to work."

"I see. Come closer. Sit."

He patted the bed next to him. My eyes flicked over to the chair, but I found myself heading toward him. Before I could decide whether to obey his command, he reached out and grabbed my hand to draw me in directly next to him.

"I can't stay long," I breathed out, my heart racing. "Your mom said you were asking for me."

"Yes. I needed to see you. I like you here. With me."

"Why?"

Multiple expressions flashed while he slid his fingers through mine, rubbing the digits in a slow, drawn out caress. I licked my lips, trying to calm the growing excitement, but I would have been lying to myself if I said there wasn't fear. It left me shaking. Confused.

"I don't know. It's you. I think, maybe, it's always been you."

Quickly, my head shook. "Your mom thinks it's Jeff you really need. She didn't want me to come. She told him to keep me away from you."

Anger had his head cocking to the side, but it was shadowed by something else. "But you came to me anyway. You wanted to see me."

"Well, yes, but—"

His other hand slid through my hair, cutting me off. I couldn't think. Couldn't do anything but stare into his hazel eyes. When his lips brushed mine, the world spun around me. My entire body shook, and I couldn't decide whether I wanted to kiss him more or run. I had always been consumed by Boston. But Jeff's fear...*that was real*.

"So good," he breathed against my lips. "If I never did this, I always wanted to. I may not remember my past, but I know what I feel: *you*." He kissed me again. This time, with more heat. Fingers tightened in my hair and Boston's tongue plunged into my mouth, sliding against mine. A moan tore from me before I could stop it. I'd kissed a boy once, but not like this. And he wasn't Boston. The man who once ruled my world was giving me what I'd always dreamed of. But at what cost?

"Wait." My chest rose and fell with each pant. I was tingling all over and couldn't stop from squirming at the arousal. It hit so hard, nothing was starting to matter. It was erasing the anxiety. Eliminating any concern I should have felt. The sensations were addicting. I wanted more. "We should talk. My brother won't like this."

"What do you want?"

He still had my head, trapping me from moving back. My mouth opened, but speaking was impossible. All I could do was stare into his depths. I knew what I wanted. What I had always wanted.

"You are so beautiful." His thumb moved over, tracing my lower lip. The captivating look on his face was like nothing I had ever seen. It lured me in. Gave me hope I could have never imagined. "What do you want, Little Lucy? Me? Do you want me?"

"B-Boston."

"God, *the way you say my name.* Tell me you want me. I have to hear you say it."

"I've always…but…"

"There are no 'buts' where you and I are concerned. It's black or white. Yes or no. Always or never…*and you said always.* You can't take that back. I refuse to let you."

He moved back in, kissing me so deep, I was no longer the Lucy I knew. I was nothing but his. The girl in me shattered, dying with each suck and nibble against my bottom lip. A new Lucy who yearned for things she didn't understand emerged. One who loved him a million times more than she ever had. When my eyes finally opened, he was staring at me. He wanted more. Lust was written all over his face. It was in the heaviness of his lids. In the way his tongue swept over his full lips, needing to taste more of me. In the way he hungrily stared at mine.

"Boston, there's something you need to know. Jeff…told me things. They scare me. He won't be okay with this. I would be in so much trouble if he knew I was even around you."

"What did he say?"

Hesitating, I turned the conversation around, despite wanting to continue. "Have you remembered anything? Maybe something about a cabin?"

Boston removed his hand from my head and faced forward, blinking repeatedly as he seemed to recall memories.

"Jeff…we were making a movie there. About a girl. I think we killed her. In the movie," he added quickly. "That's all I really remember."

"It was part of the movie?" My mouth opened through the surprise, and anger flooded in. Of course. But how had Jeff taken it so wrong? Had his mind somehow warped the truth to justify and cope with what he'd done to Boston? That had to be it. "He doesn't think it was part of the movie. Jeff truly believes you both killed a girl. And before he hit you in the head with the axe, he said he was protecting himself…from you."

"But I had a camera. My mother told me I did. I was recording. Why would I do that if I was trying to kill him? What did he have to be afraid of? It's not like I would have used the camera as some type of weapon."

"I don't know. I just know what he told me."

Boston angled himself back toward me. "I'll talk to him. Just…" His hand rose to cup my cheek and I could tell he wanted to kiss me again. "I don't want him to come between us. I want to keep seeing you."

Perplexity piqued. My mind almost couldn't believe this was happening. I still wasn't sure it was. I kept waiting for the old Boston to return. For him to pull back and say he'd made a mistake.

"Lucy." He scooted closer, once again licking his lips. But it wasn't enough. He grabbed my hip, bringing us nearly against one another. My mouth parted, and he took advantage, sweeping in to taste me. A deep sound tore from Boston, the vibrations humming through my entire body. I barely recalled clutching his shirt as he held one hand on the back of my head and the other on the middle of my back.

Drawing me in, his fingers dug into my side. I gasped, letting my tongue plunge in to meet his.

"Fuck, this is right. I knew. I just knew. Even amnesia couldn't steal you from me."

Boston reached down, gripping one side of my ass to pull me to straddle him. I didn't fight the fear. And I was afraid. I'd never gone this far with a guy. The need was never there. I had dedicated myself to a man I never thought myself capable of having.

"You're going to wake up for real and know…you're going to remember, and you're going to see this isn't what you wanted."

"Wrong." Pain sliced through my scalp as he tugged hard. The cry that left me turned into a moan as he sucked against my neck. My hips rocked, and I gripped the back of his neck as his teeth grazed my skin. *And I was gone…* The need consuming me was overwhelming. I kept moving. Kept whimpering for desires I didn't know how to fulfill.

"I want you to stay the night with me."

"W-What? Here?"

"No, we'll leave. We'll go back to my place. My mom said I live in their guest house. We'll go there."

My head shook while I scrambled from his lap. Heat burned into my cheeks, working its way down my entire body. I couldn't keep my legs still. Stopping almost felt like a new form of suffering—one I'd never experienced.

"You shouldn't leave early. This," I gestured between us, "can wait. Your health is more important. They have to make sure you're okay. I'm not sure we—you're going to change your—"

"*Never.* Come back. Right here." Boston patted his lap, and I didn't miss the hardness of his cock through the sweatpants. The inferno grew as my head snapped up. A chuckle left him, and he stood enough to reach out and pull me back. "My health is fine. They're letting me out in the next day or so anyway. You're just scared." His tone dropped—deep, coaxing, smooth. "Don't be afraid of me. I don't need memories to know innocence when I see it. I'm not going to hurt you, Lucy."

Boston gripped behind my knee, drawing it in to bend on the bed. When he brought up the other, I didn't have time to be shy. He stole the emotion with his possessive kiss. Sensations and need exploded back through and I was rocking again, holding him so tight, I was sure no one would have been able to pry me away. How long had I wanted this? Him? I was so worried he'd change his mind, I was afraid to face that he might not.

"Leave with me. *Stay with me.*"

"I really shouldn't. Jeff—"

"Is not our concern. Stay. Tonight. Tomorrow. Every day. Me and you. I want to know everything about you." He inhaled deeply, sinking his teeth into the junction at my neck as he sucked hard.

"This isn't happening."

"Wrong again, Little Lucy. This *is* happening. And no one is going to come between that.

Chapter 5
Boston

Muffled sounds—heavenly sounds. They filled the room, feeding my actions and driving me higher as I ground my cock against Lucy's hot pussy. Fuck, she was on fire. Her hips rocked, and I met her movements with a smooth thrust. We were so in sync. So perfectly made for each other. It was obvious she wanted me. And I would have done anything to keep her with me. Anything. My brain was on overload—Lucy, Lucy. Mine. Forever.

I didn't know her. Not in the way one probably should, but that didn't matter. Time was irrelevant when compared to my intuition. Lucy belonged to me. She was the only thing vital to my existence.

"Say you'll come."

"To your place?"

At my nod, she seemed to sober. Her mouth twisted, but her hips still shifted, bringing her closer.

"How will we get there? You live outside of town. I only have my bike."

And now *I* was clear-headed. Even if we did leave, I didn't have a car or money. Not here. Calling my mom didn't seem right. And I didn't have her number regardless. The nurses might.

"You said you're leaving soon. Stay at the hospital. I need time to process this anyway. I've never…and you…we've never—"

The flush tinting her cheeks brightened as she stopped. Just the sight was enough to drive me insane for more. I buried my nose in her neck and breathed in so deep, I prayed her scent would burn into my brain forever. It was familiar for reasons I didn't know. Something tried to come, but wouldn't. Had I done this before?

"If you want me to stay, I will. On one condition."

Lucy's fingers dug into my back as I nibbled on her ear. She was rocking again. And so was I. We couldn't get enough of each other.

"What?"

"I want to touch you."

Confusion masked her face, but didn't last as I drove my mouth back to hers. When the button of her jeans gave way under my fingers, she jumped. My movements were slow. I eased down the zipper, sliding my arm to pull her waist higher.

"Boston, I don't know. I…"

"Shhh. You'll like this. Trust me."

Trembling shook Lucy, but she rose to her knees, allowing me easier access. My eyes lifted to meet hers while my fingers dipped into her panties. Unbelievable wetness met my fingertips and my cock jerked. The throbbing increased as I moved in circles over her clit and folds. She was so swollen. So hot. And it was all for me. *Me.*

"God." She pushed her hands through my short hair, hovering just above my lips, her hips gyrating more. "Boston."

"I told you. I can give you this. *I can give you everything.*"

One of my digits dipped into her entrance, and Lucy gasped, pushing down even more. There was a desperation in her that fed my own. Already, I could tell she was close. It was a victory and an end I wasn't ready for. But hell if I could stop.

"Yes. This…I like this."

Applying pressure to her clit with my palm, I let her control the speed. Her pussy gripping tightly to my finger and I couldn't stop myself from sliding in another to stretch her. Nails sunk into the back of my head, moving as she held on. I was dying to fuck her. And killing myself by not acting on it.

"W-Wait. Boston."

"Remember, trust me. Keep going. Give this to me."

Lucy's sweet taste engulfed me once more. I applied more pressure, easing my fingers against her channel as her pace increased. She was taking more of me. Riding my digits like she was fucking my cock. My palm rotated, adding friction, and she shattered, spasming and crying in my mouth. I could have come at the sound. It was a melody that was only mine—one I would make sure never belonged to anyone else.

"When we get home, I'm going to do this all the time. I'll live off you—your pussy, your taste."

She was slowing, practically dead-weight on top of me as she rested her head against my neck. Pulling my fingers free, I closed my eyes and slid them into my mouth. Her essence swept over my tongue—ending me. My heart seemed to stop and visions exploded, taking her away.

But not for long.

I was walking, and it was dark. I was in a room—her room. Lucy was sleeping. Jeff was drunk and passed out. So was her mother. No one would ever know.

A sigh left her as I approached. One leg was out of the blankets while the other was hidden from view. Her little shorts V'd up her ass, making me instantly hard.

How long had I waited to come to her? Hours? All fucking day? Every day? Yes, each second was a lifetime until these stolen moments.

Her blonde hair fanned out over the pillow, and my fingers hovered above it. I lowered to my knees, leaning in and inhaling deeply. The same cheap strawberry shampoo in her bathroom filled my senses. My hand went down farther while I fingered the material of the strap to her tank top. It took everything in me not to pull it down. I wanted to see what I fantasized about. She didn't have overly big breasts, but they were getting bigger with her age. What did they look like? What would their weight feel like in my palm?

Lower, I traveled, moving my head down as I did. Inches from her thighs wasn't enough. I inhaled her scent like I always did, wanting to bask in her pussy in any way I could. It killed me not to do more. Not to wake her and act out what I'd exhausted in my mind. It was always the same. Stolen moments. *Stolen. Stolen.* Yes, I'd thought of sweeping her away, but someone…a doctor…Dr. Patron…told me she didn't deserve a life like that. Lucy would love me. Marry me. Be mine in every way if I waited and did this right. As for taking advantage of her while she slept… At her age, I knew it was wrong, but that was irrelevant. She belonged to me. Always had.

A small whimper had me freezing. Her shorts rode up, making her panties visible, and I reached out to move them to the side. I was so close. So fucking close.

"B—oston?"

Just a whisper. A dream.

I bit my lip, lifting the cotton away from her skin. Her pussy was right before my face. My eyes closed. My lungs expanded to the max through my vast inhale. Heaven—mouth-water heaven.

Braving the worst, I applied pressure with my hand against the side of her ass and eased her folds apart. Her channel opened the smallest amount, and I clenched my teeth at the desire to do more. Slowly, I lowered, only to open her entrance again. By the fourth time, she was growing so wet. I kept breathing her in, wishing, hoping. But what I wanted, I couldn't have. If I licked over her juices, she'd wake up. I couldn't risk that yet. It wasn't time. It was never time. Almost every fucking night for years—denied.

The pad of my thumb traced over her pussy as lightly as I could manage. I fixed her shorts, leaving the room as fast as I could. My thumb was already in my mouth and I was heading to the one place that would give me some sort of satisfaction: her shower, her soap, and now, with her taste.

"Are you okay? Boston?"

I blinked the colors away, removing my fingers from my mouth. I didn't answer. I was spinning Lucy, putting her on her back as I settled my weight on top.

"I saw you. I was right."

More, I kissed her. She didn't push me up or try to wiggle out from beneath me. Lucy's arms wrapped around my neck, and I did what I had always fantasized about doing.

"I want to see." Easing up her shirt, I let her adjust as the material rose higher. She stiffened a little, and her cheeks took on that pretty, rosy tint. She was embarrassed or scared, but I didn't stop. The soft fabric settled on her chest, and I brought up her bra to reveal her breasts. The pink nipples tightened, drawing me in as I dove down to suck one of the hard nubs into my mouth. What sounded like a cry left her, but Lucy's legs drew up at my sides. Regardless of the orgasm she'd just had, her body was far from sated.

"We should stop. Someone might come in."

"It's late," I said, continuing. "No one's coming, and if they do, I'll make them leave. Touch me, Lucy."

I reached for her hand, lifting as I led it into my sweatpants. *Terror.* Big green eyes looked up at me in fear as I wrapped her hand around my cock and added pressure against her fingers. My hips eased back and a groan tore from my lips as her palm slid over the head and glided along my length. Kissing her and moving back in to pinch her nipple seemed to calm the wildness within. Her body reacted, responding to my rhythm and quickening in pace as I breathed heavily through my thrusts.

"Fuck, that feels so good. You have no idea what you do to me."

My cock thickened, aching as the pressure built inside. Faster, I thrust, reaching down to cup her pussy as I used all my strength to hold myself up. Spinning had the room swaying, but I didn't stop. I couldn't. The harder I kissed Lucy, the more I was hers. Sweat covered my body. I was getting close.

"Do you wish you were…"

"Here?" My fingers rubbed harder through the jeans covering her pussy. Lucy gasped, moaning and nodding her head.

"I don't need to wish. I'm going to be. Maybe not tonight," I grunted, forcing the words out. "Maybe not tomorrow. But eventually, all of you will be mine."

Lucy's fingers dipped lower, brushing against my sac. Cupping and swirling her digits along my balls. The moment she took hold of my length and stroked back toward the tip, I came undone. Cum shot from me so hard, it sprayed across her stomach, breasts, and shirt. And it didn't seem to want to stop. My head dropped, and I tried not to collapse on top of her as I rolled to the side. I barely managed to get my shirt off to wipe her down before I locked my arms around her.

"You're staying. I want you to stay."

The room was still whirling from the overexertion. Sleep beckoned, and with each blink, my eyes were harder to reopen. She was trying to fix her pants and shirt in my firm hold, but I was too afraid she'd leave if I loosened. Darkness. I couldn't remember the last time I'd had more than a few hours here and there since I'd awoken. Lucy stayed on my mind. She haunted my dreams and every waking minute. *But I had her now.* My mind knew that and was shutting down because of it. She'd stay. I wouldn't let go. She'd stay.

Chapter 6
Lucy

    I meant to head home. I really did, but the comfort I found in Boston's arms was too good to leave. I drifted in and out of sleep, more at peace than I had ever been. *One more hour*, I kept telling myself. *One more.*
    He held me securely, resting his chin on top of my head. His light snores made their way into my dreams—dreams that weren't much different than reality. We were together, and he was holding me. Slowly, I blinked, seeing his chest not inches away. A smile pulled at my lips, and my head tilted as I gazed up at his face. A handsome face—a bloody face.
    I reared back, fighting to sit. The action caused his arms to tighten, hindering me from getting far. From what I could see, there was no wound. My hand shot up, smearing through the crimson, looking for a gash or cut from the axe. He was hurt. He—
    Wooden walls surrounded me. The room was small. Old. Mold nearly suffocated me and I fought against his grip as a multitude of knives and weapons came into view lining the walls. My eyes went to Boston, but it wasn't him anymore. It was Jeff, and he was holding me tightly as my horror grew. He was covered in blood…my blood. Lacerations were jagged over my bare chest, open and gaping. Exposed bone between my breasts had me screaming. I fought even harder, getting nowhere. Jeff was yelling at me, laughing, holding tighter as he whispered and licked over the exposed muscle of my shoulder. It wasn't right…*but I wasn't me*. I was a girl. A girl who looked like me—who, I didn't know.
    "Let me go. Let me go!"
    No response. He either didn't hear me or wasn't listening. More blood streaked over his nose and cheek, then

his forehead, as he nuzzled into me. I kept struggling. Kept begging.

"Please! Jeff! I want to leave. I want to go home!"
Nothing.
Time stretched out and weakness had my eyes drooping. I was losing too much blood. Distress kept me holding on, but it was almost impossible for me to lift my arms. I wedged them between us, using everything I had to push.
"Lucy. *Lucy.*"
I jolted, slamming my fists into Boston's chest as he stared at me. He was still holding me...tightly. One arm was hooked under my neck, gripping my shoulder, while he stroked my hair with his other hand.
"Shhh. It's okay. You were having a bad dream."
"Yes." Tears welled and my shoulders caved in at the sob wanting to escape. "I should go."
"Wait. Was it about me?"
I let my eyes drop before I shook my head. "Not really. It started off with you, but...Jeff."
At the mention, his face hardened. "But the part with me...are you afraid of me?"
"No. I mean, not anymore. I was when I thought Jeff was telling the truth."
"But he wasn't." His finger dipped under my chin, bringing me back to face him. "Listen to me, Lucy. He wasn't telling the truth. I don't know what's wrong with your brother, but it wasn't real. Kill someone? You can't think I'm capable of something like that."
"I don't. I swear I don't."
"Good."
Fingers slid up my jaw, moving back into my hair as Boston drew me in even more. My eyes closed and I breathed through the racing of my pulse. It was still hammering away. I trembled, forcing the dream to disappear. It wasn't real—this was.

"I really should be going. It has to be close to morning."

Before Boston could respond, a bang sounded from behind me. I jumped, jerking my head to look over my shoulder. Jeff was glaring, panting as he stomped in our direction. I spun to leave the bed, but Boston was too fast. His arm looped around my waist and he pulled me with him as he rose on the other side of the bed.

"Let go of her, or God help me…"

"Jeff, please."

"Shut up, Lucy! How could you? After what I told you he did?"

"He didn't do anything. I told you, Rhonda's not dead. What you said happened *isn't real*."

"It is!" His hand shot up, turning into a fist. "We're done talking. Get your ass over here right now. We're leaving."

Boston stepped in front of me, staying silent as he stared ahead. Jeff was only a few feet away, pacing. He looked ready to spring, and my tears rolled free as I battled over what to do.

"Jeff, you're sick. You feel guilty, but what happened to Boston was my fault. If I would've stayed hidden, I wouldn't have distracted the two of you. Please. I don't want you to be mad or afraid of him anymore."

"Now, Lucy!"

I side-stepped, but Boston moved with me. His arm stayed angled back, blocking any path for me to walk. We were trapped between the bed and the wall. The only way for me to get around was to climb back over the bed.

"She's not leaving."

"Excuse me?" Jeff took a step forward, and a nurse swept into the room, but left just as fast. My gut told me this was about to get bad—worse than I could imagine if I didn't do something.

"You heard me. Lucy's staying with me now. She's not safe around you. You hit her. I know you do."

"Not safe around me? She's not safe around you!" Jeff lunged, crashing into Boston. He swung, but I couldn't see the damage as they plowed into me, sending me flying into the wall. Growls and yells echoed through the wavering sounds. I was going down, but focusing was impossible from the numbing heat at the back of my head. Colors weaved together—Boston and Jeff trading punches. They were rolling on the bed one minute, and the floor the next. More people. *Security*. Everything was happening so fast, yet so slow as men pulled them apart.

They had Jeff's flailing body. He was still yelling, but whatever he was saying…it didn't make sense.

"Lucy?" My head bobbed, and Boston was suddenly before me, supporting my face. "Lucy, Jesus, stay awake, baby."

Numbness follow the swipe of his fingers under my nose and pain flared. Red. *Blood.* It coated his fingertips. I barely recalled the connection of one of their elbows to my nose. It was my head that hurt the worst, robbing me of concern from other injuries.

"I'm okay. I just—"

"Mr. Marks? Boston?"

Boston turned as a nurse and doctor entered, and lifted me to stand as they began assessing the damage. Light flashed in my eyes. More words.

"Pretty good knot you have coming up back there." More probing of my head from the doctor. "Maybe a minor concussion, but I think you'll be okay with some rest."

The doctor was suddenly dabbing my nose, then stepped back. Mrs. Marks was in the room now, though I wasn't sure when she'd arrived. Daylight broke through the cracks in the blinds. Morning. I had slept longer than I thought.

"We're leaving," Boston bit out to the doctor. "Do whatever you have to do regarding me, but I'm going home."

"We have a few more tests we'd like—"

"No. I'm fine. I said we're leaving."

"Honey."

At Boston's glare, his mother grew quiet.

"If you insist, Mr. Marks, but I must warn you against it."

"You warned. I decline any further treatment. End of story."

A silent hesitation had everyone standing still. Finally, the doctor let out a long sigh. "As you wish. I advise you be brought in if there's any change in your physical or mental state. It can take months, even years, to see—"

"I don't care. I'm fine."

The doctor left with a shake of disappointment. The pounding in my head was growing worse. I just wanted to close my eyes. Minutes went by as a nurse came and went. I found myself standing, not sure why.

Concussion.

"Where'd they take Jeff?"

Boston's hand paused as he looked up from the paper he was signing. "He'll be fine. Right now, I'm worried about you. Almost done. Then we'll go home."

Home. I probably should go home. I was going to be in so much trouble. I almost didn't want to return to face it.

"You okay? Here, take my hand."

Boston laced his fingers through mine and we were suddenly following Mrs. Marks out. Then, we had my bike loaded up, and we were driving. But not toward my home. We were going in the opposite direction, away from town.

"You don't look okay, sweetie. How are you?"

My eyes rose to look at Boston's mom's in the rearview mirror. Hazel eyes, like his. There was something in them I couldn't read. Something that gave me pause.

"My head hurts, but I'm okay. Where are we going?"

"Home. I'm going to take good care of you." Boston was sitting in the backseat of the SUV with me, stroking my hair…*soothing me.* Had he even looked away since we started driving? Every time I glanced over, he was watching me, touching my neck or jawline.

I shifted in my seat as reality began to sink in. The looming trees were a blur of green ahead. I swayed with the movement of the roads, and Boston wrapped his arm around me, resting my head on his chest. I tried to ignore the way his mother was watching us. The unease kept me quiet. She hadn't wanted me to come to Boston.

Minutes went by, and soon, we came to a road I knew all too well. I'd only seen his house a handful of times when Jeff was dropping him off, but the grandeur was enough to keep my feet rooted to the pavement as he helped me out. The large two-story cabin was more of a mansion than a home. Large glass windows covered the entire length of both floors, and a large chandelier hung in the center. It was rustic elegance at its finest.

"This way."

Boston led me off to the far side of the driveway to a two-story home a quarter of the size. The wood was the same, but there were no large windows like the main house.

The door opened at his turn and he helped me up the stairs into an open room larger than my entire house. A bed was in the far corner, with a kitchen off to the side of the enormous living room. In the middle sat an L-shaped black leather sofa centered next to an elaborate fireplace. I wasn't sure who was more surprised: me or Boston. We just stood there, staring at the splendor.

"I don't remember any of this," he breathed out. "Not even the drive here. This doesn't feel like home."

"You had an apartment down the road from my house. I don't think you've lived here in years."

"My mom said I had just moved there." Confusion drew in his features, but he pushed it away as he led me to the bed and pulled the covers back. I slid off my shoes and paused as he began to take off his pants. "First, we shower. Then, it's me and you.

Chapter 7
Boston

The warm water beating against my back didn't compare to the heat pouring from my skin. Lucy held her chest, covering her breasts, while bowing her head. Water dripped from her freshly washed hair and she shivered from the distance she had put between us in the large stand-up shower. I meant to let her adjust to the entire situation, but I couldn't stop myself from reaching forward to bring her closer.

Manipulation twisted my thoughts. She needed time...*time*, my brain screamed. I didn't listen.

"You're cold. Is modesty worth freezing to death?"

I turned, placing her in the stream. Green eyes peeked up when I grasped her wrists and brought her arms down to her side. She was breathing so heavily. She was afraid, and something in that drove me to want her more.

"There, see. That's better, isn't it?"

"Yes."

The innocence shone through with every look, every press of her thighs. Weight settled into my palm, and I gently squeezed, brushing my thumb over her nipple. Lucy's breath caught, hardening my cock until it ached.

"Do you know how beautiful you are to me?"

My hand traveled down her ribs, stopping at her waist. At my lead, she stepped in. The water had her breasts gliding against me, and I tightened my hold as her fingers brushed against my side.

"I don't understand why you never said anything before. I feel like this isn't real."

"I think there are many reasons. Most importantly, we have quite the age gap between us, don't we."

It wasn't a question, but she nodded. "Yes."

"And I could have gotten in a lot of trouble for that, right?"

"Yes."

"*But not anymore.* Nothing can keep us apart now." My thumb pushed into her stomach. Lower, I moved, waiting for her to tell me to stop. When she didn't, I dipped lower, settling the pads of my fingers at the top of her slit.

"I'm scared."

"There's nothing to fear. Nothing at all."

Slick wetness met me as I glided to her entrance and traced around the opening. Inching in, I moved my digit to my mouth. Tasting her wasn't just a want. *I had to.* I couldn't resist the agonistic longing to have her in me. To make her part of me. To have her engulf so much of who I was, air no longer controlled my sense of smell, her essence did. The battle was real, and when it came to Lucy, control or common sense would never win.

"Fucking God help me."

I was already pushing her back against the wall and dropping to my knees.

"Boston, wait. *Boston!*" Hands pushed hard into my shoulders and a squeal filled the space as my head wedged between her closing thighs. Lucy went wild trying to break free, but I only forced her legs apart harder. My hand shot to her neck, pinning her, and my fingers spanned over the column of her throat. *Thump-thump Thump-thump.* Her pulse was racing—hammering with such force, it drowned out my own.

When my tongue traced through her folds, she cried out, on the verge of tears. "Please. You have to stop." All her strength leveled against my forehead as she tried to push me back. My eyes shot up to meet hers, and she froze. Lucy was conflicted, and probably as inexperienced as I was. I couldn't see being with anyone else. I wouldn't have done that to her or myself. What I needed came natural. Whether it was instinct or forgotten knowledge from my past, I hadn't a clue.

"This is wrong. You shouldn't be—"

"No, baby, this is *more* than right. I want you. Let me show you how much. Let me make you feel good."

I sucked her juices from her folds, moving toward her entrance at a leisurely pace. My hand dropped to her breast, rolling her nipple, pinching as she got wetter. By the time I made it to her channel, Lucy's mouth was open and her eyes were wide. Fingers spread over my head and she drew them in, clutching my hair while her moans echoed around us.

"That's it. Let yourself enjoy this. Love it, because I do."

"It feels good, but…wrong."

"It's not. Nothing is wrong when it comes to us."

Pulling back, I made a path to her clit, flicking over the sensitive nerves before adding suction. Sounds grew louder, adding to the weight in my chest—to the black hole that seemed to be growing by the second. Any sense of myself I had disappeared, and she was taking its place.

Suck, flick, suck, flick. I moved down, fucking her with my tongue before heading back to her clit. I let time sweep by, thriving in how she consumed me with every breath.

"Boston. God."

"Don't come yet, baby. Not yet."

I stood, teasing her with my fingers before I could force myself into action. Turning off the water, I pulled her to the bed. When I had her lying down, my face was back between her legs. Wetness flourished, and I added one finger, inserting the second almost just as fast. It didn't take long to taste how close she was. When I rose, covering her body with mine, Lucy hungrily met my mouth.

"Spread wider for me."

"It's going to hurt."

"A little, but I promise it'll feel so good, you won't even remember the pain."

"How do you know?"

I grew silent, unsure. Words came, and they were the only thing that made sense. "I'd never hurt you if I didn't know I could make it better in the end. You'll love this. I won't stop until you do."

My length moved against her wet slit and Lucy's legs hesitantly widened. It wasn't long before she rocked, digging into my back from the pleasure. When I grabbed the base of my cock and eased the tip into her channel, she tensed.

"Not yet," I whispered against her lips. "Get use to me. Feel me stretch you."

The head of my cock wasn't even in all the way. Tightness gripped my tip and I withdrew completely, only to use her wetness to sink in deeper.

"That's it. Love it, Lucy. Love how I feel inside you."

Again, I withdrew, moving to my knees and lifting hers toward her chest. My cock fit against her pussy, and I watched her envelop me as I eased forward. She was trembling, but moaning at the slow thrusts. I paused, panting as sweat began to cover me. The head of my cock was being gripped like a vice and I couldn't get enough. I leaned forward, positioning myself over her as we came face to face.

"Hold on to me. Kiss me. Whatever you do, don't stop."

My lips crushed into hers, and I rotated my hips, surging forward to break through her wall. A scream left Lucy's mouth, and I froze. She was writhing, trying to push me off, but I wasn't letting her. Instead, I eased out enough to make her calm, then slowly inched in even more, repeating the process. Still, I kissed her through the sobs. When I reached between us and applied pressure to the top of her slit, she changed.

"Better?"

Lucy sniffled, nodding. Parting her lips, she let out something between a whimper and a sweet sigh. Her body relaxed while she arched her hips, taking me all the way.

Thrust after thrust, her impatience grew. Nails dug into my back, and I moved over her clit faster.

"Look at me, baby. Don't close your eyes. *See me.*"

It was more than having her attention. Lucy had to see how much I wanted this—*her*. And I had to remember every expression she made through a moment I had torturously longed for. I couldn't remember the wait, but my subconscious did, and the pain associated with my forgotten memories held more yearning and sadness than I could bear.

"I've always seen you." Her fingers grasped onto both sides of my face while I pounded into her. "O-Only you. *Boston.*"

The words died out as Lucy's body jerked and her legs kicked out. Pleasure drew her forehead in and her mouth slightly parted. The sweet scream brought my mouth down to hers. Even with my eyes closed, I held to our moment. I focused on nothing but the beautiful mental snapshot as it mingled with her taste. Time sealed in my mind, cherishing every second, remembering this as I kissed her with everything I had.

Control slipped away as I lost myself in Lucy. I made love to her with every uncontrollable ounce of obsession I harbored. And the more she kept my stare, the more I unraveled. My cock swelled and flashes came as my cum shot deep into her. Another doctor. A different one. A procedure planned long before so I'd never have to share her with anyone else. Not even a child. *A vasectomy.*

****

"I said no. I don't care if Jeff's worried about her. He's fucking crazy, Mother. Did you know he told Lucy I killed someone? Me! It was the entire reason she was staying away from me. If she wouldn't have discovered he was lying, I wouldn't have her now. I'm not giving her back. She's eighteen. She can make up her own mind, *and she chooses me.*"

I flexed my fingers at the weight of the grocery bags my mother had handed over. The anger thrumming through me was worse than when Jeff and I fought at the hospital.

He'd already sent the cops over, but there was nothing they could do. Once they saw Lucy was okay, their hands were tied, and they left. Now, he was stalking my mother, trying to get her to convince Lucy to go home.

Lucy not safe. Like I would hurt her.

Whispers echoed in my head. *Lies.* I was capable of hurting people. Never her, but people. The memories, the blood, the men, chasing someone…they were movies. They weren't real.

Why didn't I entirely believe that?

"All I'm saying is you should let her know her brother is worried. What she decides will be up to her. She can still choose you and not stay here, Boston. She's young, and you just woke up from a horrible accident and coma. I think the three of you—Jeff, you, and Lucy—need to work this out and come to terms."

My mouth twisted as I pulled up the bags. "Thanks for the groceries. It was very nice of you. I appreciate it, but there's nothing to work out. Lucy stays."

I turned, pausing as I caught Lucy's stare through the upstairs window. Racing exploded in my chest, half-anger, half-dread. By the time I got to the top of the stairs, she was already dressed and waiting. Two days she'd been with me, and I knew she was getting antsy to go home.

"My mother got us food. Nice of her, right?"

"Yes." Hesitation. "Boston, we need to talk."

I leaned in, pressing my lips to hers as I passed. An excuse was hard to come by, but the contents I pulled out made it easier. "Is there really anything to talk about? I guess we can discuss what movie to put on while I cook this popcorn."

She shook her head as I held it up. "Your mom said Jeff's name. I read her lips. I don't like my brother so worried. He's not okay. I think I should go home. At least long enough to figure out what I should do."

"So he can beat the hell out of you for being with me?"

"He won't. Not if I go back. He'll be glad to see me."

"Maybe for the first five minutes, but then he'll hurt you. After that, he'll try to keep you away from me. We both know he will. Then what? Pretend this didn't happen? Try to keep this a secret? Bullshit. I won't do that, Lucy. I can't." I surged forward, pulling her into my arms and kissing her. My tongue made a slow path along hers. She started to pull back, but I didn't stop until she was holding onto me. "Don't leave. If you want to talk to him, I'll go with you and we can do it in your front yard. But stay here with me."

I gripped into her ass, sliding my cock against her stomach. In the last two days, we'd done nothing but have sex, eat, shower, and repeat. I couldn't get enough. Even now, I longed to taste and be inside her.

"I can't stay forever, Boston."

"Why not?"

Seriousness had her eyes narrowing. "You mean that?"

"Well, yeah. I don't know why I never said anything to you before, but I feel…inside…" Closing my eyes, I let out a deep breath before I could face her again. "I love you. I think I've always loved you. I made the mistake of not telling you once, and I could have died without you knowing the truth. I can't do that again. I want you to stay and be with me. Forever."

Was I expecting happiness? Excitement? Maybe a response that mirrored my own? Lucy didn't do anything but stare at me in shock.

"Say something. Anything."

"I don't know what to say. I never saw this coming. Maybe I used to hope, but—"

"Used to?"

Lucy paused, slightly wiggling in my arms. "Well, before the accident...back when you and Jeff were on good terms. Now it makes things complicated. I don't want there to be tension between everyone. I don't want my brother upset and thinking the worst of you. I want things back to the way they were."

Tears filled her eyes, triggering anger at her pain. I suppressed the emotion, making sure she saw my support instead. Even weeks out of a coma, manipulation came naturally. "If that's what you want, then that's what you'll get. I'll talk to Jeff. We'll make this work. If I can get his and your mother's support, will you stay?"

"You would do that...even after the last time you both faced each other?"

A smiled tugged at my mouth and I bit my bottom lip as violent whispers returned.

"There's nothing I wouldn't do for you, Lucy. *Nothing.*"

Chapter 8
Lucy

To say I was terrified was an understatement. And it wasn't just because Boston was driving when I didn't think he should be. The small two-seater sports car I used to dream about riding in was now a potential death trap for every hill and sharp turn we took through the surrounding forest.

As I gave him directions to my home, he grew distant. Quiet. And I was trembling worse than ever. This wasn't going to go well; I could feel it. There was no way Jeff was going to do a one-eighty and welcome the idea of me being with a supposed killer. To make it worse, I was having my own doubts about going back. I didn't know this Boston. He was constantly touching me, staring at me...*wanting me*. My girlish fantasies were changing, morphing with the woman I was becoming. I loved it. I loved him. But I was also scared of what that meant.

Our small town came into view, old buildings consisting of department stores, giftshops, and a few family owned restaurants blurring by as we passed. I pointed to a road a few blocks down.

"Take a left there."

Boston's eyes narrowed, jerking this way and that, as if he was either remembering or trying to. He nodded, hitting his blinker. My pulse hammered away, and I was shaking to the point of being sick. What was I going to do? I was confused over what was right. Maybe it was the tension. Maybe it was the story my brother fed me. The nightmares still came, transitioning from Boston's accident to either him or Jeff covered in blood.

"Right down there. The white house with the blue shutters."

"That's what I thought."

The words were barely a whisper. Boston glanced over to me, his face was full of something I couldn't recognize. It was hard, but there was…fear? Yes and no. There was something more.

"You're coming back with me, right?"

My mouth opened, but before I could answer, he stopped the car three houses down from mine.

"Lucy, you're coming back with me, aren't you?" Not just fear, desperation. It twisted my stomach, almost taking away my consent. Boston needed me. Maybe for more than I realized. Guilt. It returned. I had done this to him. I changed him that day. I changed my brother too. I came between them and ruined everything.

"Y-Yes. You have my word."

A long moment went by before he eased the car forward. We were barely parking when my brother barreled through the door, his face a mix of rage and terror. My gaze shot to Boston, who's expression was…gone. I was uncertain on what to do, but I opened the door. Immediately, my hand jerked up to ward off my brother. I didn't want him coming up to pull me in the house. That wouldn't be good for Boston to see. I wasn't sure how he'd react.

"Jeff, wait. We came here to talk."

"Nothing to talk about," he said, growing closer.

"Yes, there is. It's time we set things straight."

Boston came around the front of the car, moving in next to me. I didn't ignore the fact that the engine was still running. I felt sick, and nothing I could think to do eased the churning.

"What's there to fix, Lucy? A girl is dead and you're…what, fucking my murdering ex-best friend?"

More anger. Disgust. My face burned at the acknowledgement, but Boston pulled me in, causing Jeff to side-step like an animal debating which way to attack.

"You're mad and afraid of me. That's obvious, but, Jeff…*I didn't kill anyone*. I remember making a movie. That wasn't real. And I don't blame you for striking me with the axe. I was stupid, getting so close. That's not on you, man. Let it go." He paused. "As for Lucy…" tighter his fingers gripped into my bicep, "she's the only one I remembered when I came out of the coma. Just her. Not you, not my mother or father—her. And my feelings were obvious. Maybe they've always been there. I feel like they have. Perhaps it was our friendship that had me not acting on them. But I love her, I do, and I'm sorry, but this time, I'm not holding back."

"This isn't fucking happening. Do you see why I tried to keep you away, Lucy?" Jeff ran his hand down his face, going pale. "I know you've always had a crush on Boston, but look at me, trust me. I'm your brother. Boston is not Boston. Boston is sick. You need to come to me. Just start walking and I'll take care of the rest. Don't be afraid. *Walk.*"

Jeff was back to cutting sharp angles in the yard as he paced faster. Sweat beaded down his face, and I regretted glancing up to Boston. His eyes…they were different. Darker.

"Jeff, I promised Lucy I would try to work this out with you, so I'm going to pretend you're not trying to take her away from me. You say I killed someone. Prove it. Where's the body? Let's go find it."

I stiffened and Jeff jolted to a stop. "You knew we'd get to this point. You prepared for this!"

"What?" Boston looked between us, confused. "I've been a coma, or did I plan for that too?"

"I don't know. I…I don't know, but you knew we would get to this point. It's gone, Boston! The body is gone. It took me hours to get home. What did you do with it after I ran off? Did you bury it? Burn it?'

"Lucy?" Boston threw me a look, and I wasn't sure what to do or believe. Jeff wasn't making sense. It left the confliction worse. I had wanted a resolution, but it didn't look like I was going to get one. Before I could do much, my mother walked out. She was smiling, but it turned to worry as she came forward.

"Boston, so glad you're doing better. You look good."

"Thank you, Ms. Adams."

Her attention came back to me. "Lucy? Do you want to come in and talk?"

Fingers gripped tighter, and I let my palm settle over Boston's lower chest. "It's okay. I have to go in and get clothes anyway."

"I'll buy you new ones."

I paused. "That's absurd. I'm going to talk to my mom. I'll be right back."

"You won't. I'll go in with you."

"*Boston.*" I tried to keep calm. "Stay here or wait in the car. It'll only take me a few minutes."

He shifted, and I practically had to pry his hand off me. Jeff back-stepped, following me toward the house. My nausea was at an all-time high, and I was beyond shaking. My teeth were chattering so hard, I was sure they'd break.

The door shut behind me, and I moved in toward my mom to keep Jeff at a distance, but I wasn't so lucky. He was on my heels, following me and my mom to the table. I didn't sit down. I couldn't. I felt like I was split between two people—two different versions of myself. The good me, and the new me.

"All right. You two better start talking. What is going on? And, Lucy, don't get me wrong, I love Boston like a son, but staying away from home without letting me know is not okay. I almost went to the police. If it weren't for Jeff filling me in and Mrs. Marks coming to the diner, I would have thought you were taken. I'm on the verge of grounding you for a month."

"Do it. Ground her."

"Shut up, Jeff! Mom, Jeff says—"

"Don't, Lucy."

My eyes cut over to him and tears spilled down my cheeks. "Don't tell me what to do. This is your fault! You're sick and you need help."

"*What?*" My mom's voice had me turning back to her.

"Jeff said he and Boston killed a girl before he hit Boston with the axe. He said he was trying to defend himself, but the girl he claimed they killed isn't dead. She's alive. He…invented it all to cope with his guilt. Now he's afraid of Boston and says I can't be around him. It's not real! All he does is drink now and freak out about something that didn't happen."

"Not true! It did, goddammit!"

"Calm down," my mother exploded. "Jeff, what's this about killing a girl?"

A sob left him, and he jerked the chair from the table, collapsing into it. "I swear, Mom, I didn't want to hurt her. Boston…he's a monster. I thought we were just going to use her for the movie, but what he did…I-I didn't want to hurt her, but I didn't have a choice. He had a knife. I didn't know what to do!"

A shade of color dropped from my mother's face and she turned to me. "Why is this the first time I'm hearing about this?"

"He made me promise not to tell."

"Lucy Elaine, that is not a secret you keep. You said the girl he claimed he hurt isn't dead?"

"No. Her name is Rhonda. There was a missing poster up in the break room at the theater, but she returned with her boyfriend, pregnant. She probably doesn't even know Jeff. She's a little older than me."

My mother nodded, closing her eyes for a second longer than normal. "Okay. And what's going on between you and Boston? Do I even need to ask?"

"He says he loves her," Jeff blurted out.

My mother's eyes widened and one of her eyebrows rose. "And what about you? Do you love him?"

"I...did. I mean, I do, but..." My hand went out to Jeff, and she seemed to understand.

"And what do you plan to do?"

Lowering my head, I stared at my fingers as they tugged at the hem of my shirt. "I want to go back. We're staying at his parents' guesthouse. I'm staying there with him."

"Unbelievable. You've both known each other for most of your lives. How did I not know? How did I not see it before?"

The questions were whispered, but they had Jeff glaring over. "Because it wasn't there before. Boston didn't give a shit about Lucy until he woke up from his coma."

Anger had more tears leaving me. "You don't know that, Jeff. Just because he didn't tell you doesn't mean he didn't feel something."

"Hey. Enough. Both of you. Lucy, I think maybe you should stay here for a few weeks. You're young, and he's just recovering. If it works out in the long run, great. If not, you may be sparing yourself from a life you aren't prepared for."

"Mom!"

"Don't 'Mom' me. You're staying. And you," she turned to my brother, "we'll...talk to someone. We'll figure this out."

"There's nothing to figure out. I know what happened. I know what I saw. What I did," he said lower.

"Be that as it may, you're still going to talk to someone."

"We can't afford that."

"Jeffrey." Her voice was stern as she stared at him. "You let me worry about that, and stop arguing."

I took a step toward the door, pulling my mother's attention. She gave a quick shake of her head, and more tears left me. I was crumbling to pieces, caught between figuring out right and wrong. All I knew was what I had to do.

"Boston needs me. I love him. I *have* to go."

"Like hell!" Jeff surged to his feet, but my mother's arm shot out to push against his chest.

"Lucy, I told you what I wanted you to do. I want you to stay home and take this slow."

"And I respect that, but I'm eighteen, and I can make my own decisions. I choose to be with Boston."

She was ready to argue back, but I saw her exhaustion. Defeat had her shoulders sagging, and for the first time, I saw just how aged my mother had become. Life hadn't been easy on her. It hadn't been even before my absent father left. Now with all of this in the open, I worried whether she could handle it.

"I'm sorry, Momma. I am, but please…don't be mad at me."

"Baby, I'm not mad. I'm worried about you."

I threw myself in her arms, hugging tightly as my brother made a growling sound. "Don't worry. I'll be okay. I promise. I'll come by all the time. It'll be fine." I turned to Jeff, trying to root in my assurance. "I'll be fine."

"Yeah, sure. Until he tries to kill you."

Chapter 9
Boston

Fingers.
One.
Thwack!
Two.
Thwack!
Three.
Thwack!
More.

The hatchet felt so real in my hand—so secure as I drove it down on a man's digits. I couldn't see the woman he'd hit in my memories, but there had been one.

"Next hand."

A hollow sound whined, courtesy of his removed tongue. He turned his head, revealing the hole evident from the blond's missing ear. Half of his face was skinned, and different shades of red painted between the drying, darkened muscle. From the patches of white spots forming more toward the top, I knew I'd taken the flesh in strips over time. *The same side he'd beat her on.* Round eyes jetted from me to the ceiling. The wildness, the panic, left the one free of skin looking as though it was going to slip from the socket at any moment. I was getting better at this. I was keeping them longer. Not just for a few hours like before. *Days.* I kept them for days…

More hollow screams.
Thwack!

A gasp left me, and Lucy's yard came back into view. I tried not to believe myself capable of such bloody and grotesque acts. Maybe I was in denial. Maybe I was too afraid to believe who I *really* was. All I knew was I'd calculated at least two perfect murders. Mother and brother.

The two people closest to the woman I loved. I didn't know them, and I didn't care to. *Lucy. Lucy. Lucy.*

I was like a rabid animal, out of control and deadly if I didn't get my prey. To think of Lucy as my victim was odd. I didn't understand it, but I didn't understand myself either. She drove me. She moved me. Her hair, the scent of her skin, the way her curves felt under my palm, my fingers—around my fingers as I buried them inside her…her moans. I wasn't even a person; I was a vessel of obsession made just for her. Perhaps I truly did expire when that axe embedded in my skull. Without Lucy, I didn't exist. I didn't want to. It was her or nothing. No price was too high to keep it that way.

The door opened and I stopped walking the length of my car as she came out carrying a duffle bag. I rushed forward, not sure whether to kiss her or carry her to the car so we could leave this place—these dark thoughts.

"Lucy, wait."

Her mother rushed out behind her, and I fought the urge to lunge and make her continue to the car. Instead, I plastered a weak smile on my face while I walked around to her side. Green eyes, the same color as Lucy's, came to me, and a slight familiarity stirred.

"You both be safe. My door is always open. You know that."

There was some hidden message she didn't want me to grasp, but I caught it just fine. With Jeff spouting off how dangerous I was, there was no doubt her mother knew. Blistering heat bubbled, and I grabbed Lucy's bag—subtle, but defining.

"Lucy is in good hands, Ms. Adams."

"Katherine," she offered.

I nodded as she wrapped her arms around Lucy, whispering something in her ear I couldn't hear. When Lucy broke away, she swiped away her tears. From how bloodshot her eyes were, I knew she'd been crying before now. A lot.

"Take care of Jeff, Momma. He's not okay. I'll be back in a few days to check in."

"Visit soon. And...don't forget about work," her mom rushed out. "Sarah's been lenient under the circumstances. Try to get back soon."

"I will."

Jeff stepped from the threshold, eyeing me. Our stares met, and there was no hiding our disdain. He was going to fuck this up; I could feel it.

"I'll make sure she goes." Pushing my fingers through Lucy's, I led her back to the car. She threw a wave, but got in without any more incident.

"Nothing better happen to her, Boston. *Nothing.* Do you hear me!"

I paused outside my door, watching as Jeff stepped up next to his mother. Movement registered in my peripheral from their neighbors, and my mind slowed. Calculations clicked—swift, flawless.

"I love Lucy. She means everything to me." Dramatic pause. A deep sigh. A sad expression. "Please get help, Jeff. I miss my best friend." I turned to his mother, making my nervousness over Jeff obvious. "Don't hesitate to contact me if you need anything, Ms. Adams. Katherine. I'll help any way I can."

I got in the car while an odd sense of self rolled through me. It had me staring ahead, searching for some type of emotion to go along with it. But nothing was there. Just acceptance. I wasn't a good man. And not just bad, but beyond that. I was smart. I was devious. *I was deadly.*

****

"Faster." I weaved through the trees, feeling stronger than ever. Lucy was running. Blonde hair spun out around as she stole a glance behind her, but she pushed herself harder as I closed in. "Come on, baby. Faster! If I get you, you know what's going to happen."

A squeal echoed through the trees and the frigid air burned my lungs, driving me at a speed that was exhilarating. Details, my senses—everything heightened to degrees that amazed me. Despite the excitement, there was a calmness.

I eyed her location, driving myself faster as I took a wider path. She cut to the right, and my feet slid against the dirt and foliage as I broke hard and barreled toward her. A piercing scream tore from her and I laughed, tackling her down, hard. The impact was jarring, but I thrived in the pain, guarding her like a treasure as I eased her fall with my body. It was unlike anything when it mixed with the spike of fear she held.

We both laughed, and my lips crushed into hers as I pinned her wrists down.

"Did you really think I'd let you get away? You know what this means, right?"

Pants left her as she tried to catch her breath. What started out as a game of basketball quickly escalated to her teasing me as she moved her ass against me. I tried to get the ball, but in truth, all I wanted was to throw her down and fuck her in my driveway. When my hand pressed against her lower stomach, she had slipped through and started running. Now, she was mine, and right where she needed to be.

"It means we go inside. It's freezing out here."

"I'll warm you up." I sucked against her bottom lip, biting before I plunged my tongue back in to taste her. Lucy moaned, shivering as she broke away.

"We can't. I don't have time. I'm already going to be late."

"Don't go. Stay with me."

"Boston, I've *been* staying with you," she laughed. "It's only for a few hours."

Reluctantly, I nodded. I hated when she went to work. She'd been here over a week and had spent half that time at the theater. How had I done this before? How had I ever left her side? I couldn't fathom it. Each hour dragged on forever. I counted the minutes. I paced while watching the clock. Three days—three years. That's what it felt like, and I couldn't stand it. I'd give it some time, then I'd convince her to quit.

"I was thinking, should we make a movie?"

"What sort of movie?"

I helped her up, dusting the dirt from her back and pulling a twig from her hair.

"I don't know. I've been trying to get more memories back. More...a sense of self for who I was before. It seems I used to have a passion for it...but I don't feel that pull anymore. I thought maybe if we tried, I could put more pieces of the puzzle together."

"Oh. Well, if you search inside yourself, what type comes to you?"

"Maybe a scary one. Something like me and Jeff were making."

Lucy glanced at me nervously, but picked up her pace. "I'm not sure. It didn't go very well the last time you tried. What if something happened? I wouldn't know what to do. What if—"

"It's not your fault."

Reaching for her hand, I brought her to a stop to face me. The guilt was something she led on to more than I liked. I still couldn't remember exactly how the day had progressed, but even if she had distracted me like she'd said, I had a fucking axe coming at my head. The part of me I tried to push away said it wouldn't have happened if I had been more focused. *For Lucy... For Lucy...*

She was talking, but I heard nothing—nothing but her gasp. Pain rocked me, and I was falling—smiling, falling. Her face. Blood. Red. A red Lucy as blood coated my eye. That wasn't something to smile about, but there was something. Something about that moment I couldn't remember.

"Boston?"

"What?"

"I...nothing. Let's go. I have to get ready."

The rest of the walk, I replayed the vision. Over and over, I tried to claw through the block making it impossible to decipher. Whatever I meant to accomplish that day temporarily died with me.

Lucy jolted to a stop, and I nearly plowed over her with how gone I was. Jeff was standing in the driveway by his truck, staring right at us as we came to a stop just past the tree line.

"You okay?"

A hand pushed against my stomach, signaling for me to remain. She walked forward, but I kept my place next to her.

"I'm doing good. How are you?"

A shrug was met with annoyance. "Seeing a fucking shrink for nothing, but it's whatever. Can I talk to you...*alone*?"

"Sur—"

"Nope," I cut her off, and Lucy threw me a look. "What?" I hissed. "I don't trust him."

"Me?" Jeff's anger rose. "You know what, I'm not going to keep repeating this like a fucking broken record. I don't give a shit if you have amnesia. You're a fucking murderer, and now you have my sister. Just because you're nice now doesn't mean it'll last. The old you will come back, and when you do, I'll be here, motherfucker. You even think about hurting her and your dead for good this time."

"Did you come here to threaten or fight again? *You said you wouldn't do this*," Lucy snapped.

"It's the truth. Listen...Lucy. Please. I know you don't believe me. No one does, but I'm going to prove to you what I'm saying is the truth. Take a drive with me. See this cabin he keeps hidden in the woods. There still has to be blood in there. He fucking...he cut her up so bad. I'm begging you. Please. One drive. It's not far."

"Jeff, *please, stop*."

"If we don't find anything, I'll never bring this up again. Please. Do it for me. For your brother. I need you."

After all the visions, maybe I should have been afraid. But I didn't feel fear. My reaction was one I didn't understand. A smile peeled back to expose my teeth, and without thought, I winked.

Chapter 10
Lucy

"What have you done?"

Jeff flew forward, panicked. He was breathless, appearing on the verge of some sort of episode. Wide eyes searched Boston's face, *a sad face*, and my heart dropped as my brother began to pull at his short hair.

"You covered your ass there too, didn't you? I'm not crazy. I'm not crazy!"

My hand reached forward, but Boston's arm stayed wrapped around my stomach. I wasn't sure what to do or how to help. I didn't owe him anything after what he'd done to me growing up, but he was still my brother. Seeing him so distraught didn't sit well.

"You're upsetting Lucy. I think it's time for you to go. I hate to have to do this with you being family and all, but I'm going to have to ask you not to come back until you can learn to control your…delusions."

I elbowed Boston's side, and he sighed. "Okay, mistaken truths."

"You're a piece of work. I don't know how much more of this I can take. I don't see any other way. I don't, and I guess it doesn't matter."

"What do you mean?"

Green eyes lowered to me, but he went back to Boston.

"I'm going to tell them. I'm going to turn myself in. Jail isn't worth losing my sister. And if I'm locked away, you will be too. You can't have her then, can you?"

Boston shrugged. There wasn't any guilt or fear I could detect coming from him at the threat. "Do what you have to, but don't be surprised if they lock you up in a mental institution. Come on, baby. It's getting late. You need to get ready."

"*Lucy*...? Please, I'm begging you. I'm begging you with everything I have."

The heartbreaking plea had my feet planting into the ground. I sighed, and a mix of uncertainty came with what I knew I had to do.

"I'll go see this cabin on one condition."

"Lucy," Boston growled, but I jerked myself free of his hold.

"Don't 'Lucy', me. If my brother wants to show me something that could *help* him, I'm going."

Boston's face turned to stone. For a good minute, he didn't speak. "Fine. But I'm coming."

"No, you're not," I countered. Surprise melted his mask until his eyes searched mine. Stepping forward, I placed a kiss on his cheek. "Jeff needs this. What he doesn't need is you making it harder on him. Stay. When he sees there's nothing to worry about, I'll have him bring me back. He'll have no excuse not to."

"Bullshit. He'll invent an excuse. He'll say I cleaned up the scene like he did before. I'm coming."

"*Boston*. I. Said. No."

The stunned disbelief that registered was as if I had slapped him. The pacing began—which I noticed he did when he didn't have control. Just like in the front yard at my mom's when I watched him from my window. Or at the theater last week, when he paced outside his car while he waited for me to get off work. I saw his overwhelming need not to be parted. And here it was again. Once he thought of me being out of the picture, he couldn't cope.

"Kiss me and tell me you'll see me soon," I said, calmer. "Have some trust in me."

"It's not you I don't trust." Anger dripped from each word, but he pulled me in, kissing me as his eyes cut up to my brother. They never closed, and neither did mine. When he finally pulled back, he was barely able to look at me at all. "I'll see you soon."

My hand rose, gripping firmly to the back of his neck and pulling him down so he'd face me. "Say it again. Believe it."

"Dammit, Lucy." Hesitation. "I'll see you soon. I love you."

The kiss was softer, and when he closed his eyes, so did I. Hands locked to my hips, gripping as if he were terrified to let me go. Finally, they dropped, freeing me. To wait would have been a mistake. I needed him to accept that I wasn't always going to be here. I couldn't live like that.

I turned, and Jeff headed to the driver's side while I got in the truck. When I waved and we took off, Boston stepped forward. The angles of his face were sharp, but something almost accepting softened them as he reluctantly waved back.

"You're doing the right thing, Lucy. When you see the cabin, you're never going to want to come back."

"What if there's nothing there?"

Jeff turned onto the main road, giving a fierce shake. "There has to be."

"You're bringing me back if there's not."

Repeatedly, his jaw flexed. "There will be. I know what happened."

The loud roar of the truck was the only sound between us. Jeff and I grew quiet while he drove deeper into the woods. It would be dark soon. I didn't like the idea of being in the wilderness so late. It was dangerous, and the expanse was vast. People died when they got lost, and some were experienced hikers. A few miles later, Jeff turned onto a dirt road where we proceeded to go even farther into trees.

"I'm sure this is it. I've only been back once…to look for the body," he said, glancing over. "It shouldn't be that much longer."

The truck rocked through the ruts, and I held to the door as I bounced in the seat. Jeff turned on his headlights, and just when I was sure he was lost, he turned, bringing an overgrown trail into view. Overgrown…but there.

My heart thumped hard in my chest and fear crept in as I gazed at my brother.

"This isn't going to be pretty. I know I've done some bad things in my life, but I really am sorry you're going to have to see this. It was a massacre."

My denial didn't erase the fact that, somewhere inside, I almost believed him.

Grabbing a flashlight, Jeff clicked it on. The beam lit up the floorboard, the light trembling just like we both were. When he opened the door, my hands almost felt like they were made of lead. Somehow, I forced it open. Creaking from the old hinges broke through the eerie silence and I moved in close, holding his arm as we entered the thick foliage.

"How far is the walk? It won't be light much longer."

"It's not light in there now."

Jeff led us inside at a powerwalk, and the darkness immediately closed in. With how thick the trees were, I couldn't see a foot in front of me or to either side.

"You never said how far it was."

"I'm not sure." He paused. "I haven't been able to find the cabin. I only found where I think Rhonda and I ended up before Boston found us."

"You don't know where it is?"

"I wasn't paying attention when we first headed there. The girl…she was pretty. Then, we were drinking. I don't even know how I made it home. It took me hours, Luce. Fucking forever."

Openings appeared, spanning out throughout endless space that all looked the same. Trees. More trees. Thick spots of bushes and twisting vines. A twig broke behind us, and I jumped, holding Jeff tighter.

"I think it was this way. It was a pretty good distance."

We took a right, winding through a path before Jeff stopped and turned us left, then right. We were zigzagging into oblivion, and my stomach knotted the deeper we traveled. A half-hour passed. Longer. A good hour or two more. Night, darker than black, swallowed us whole and more movement rustled not far away.

"We have to go back. We're lost."

"No. It's here. Somewhere. We'll find it. You have to see."

What sounded like a growl had both of us spinning. The light shone through nothingness and a short, dark shadow blurred low and fast through the beam.

"Jeff, I want to leave."

"Afterward, Lucy. We have to keep going."

"We can come back in the morning!"

BOOM!

Thunder sounded like a cannon and I screamed, jumping in time for lightening to cast shadows around us.

"Jeff, please!"

"A little longer. Hurry."

Even as he said it, he dragged me along. Branches tugged at my pants and scraped my face as the density thickened again.

BOOM!

FLASH.

Rain pelted against my hair. First randomly, then heavier as we went through space after space of clearing. Another sound, seemingly closer than the last. Trembling from the cold, I angled my face more toward Jeff as he interlaced us through even more nothingness.

"This isn't right. We should have been there by now."

"When? Hours ago? Jeff, face it, there is no cabin. There was no girl."

Droplets pounded the ground as he broke away from me and spun in a circle. Each shrub, every hanging limb, looked the same as the last few hundred. Light highlighted the way we'd come, and I groaned at how much my legs ached. My entire body was screaming in pain. There was no telling how far we'd covered. Walking back was unthinkable.

"This way."

"You can't be serious."

There was no anger as Jeff reached for me. He looked defeated—and it had nothing to do with the fact that we might be lost. If there was a cabin out here, he wasn't leaving until we found it.

"Fine, but you're buying me the biggest breakfast tomorrow morning. I'm talking eggs, bacon, pancakes—the works."

He laughed, glancing over at me. The smile was one I hadn't seen toward me in…maybe ever. He seemed to realize it to, his face turning stoic once more.

"After we find it, if you leave with me, I'll buy you breakfast every morning. I haven't been very nice to you. I'm sorry for that. It was wrong. It's just…life, it's hard, you know? I think I was a parent to you more than Mom or Dad ever were. I was young and Mom just kept dumping you on me. Not that it was her fault, she had to work. And Dad, he was shitty. He was never home. Then…well, that whole thing happened. You didn't know what I did about him."

"What do you mean?"

Jeff let out a long exhale. "Dad didn't just cheat on Mom, Lucy. He had another family. A daughter—Hannah. She's probably about twelve now."

"What?"

Shaking my head, I stepped back. "You're lying. Mom would have told me. *Dad* would have told me."

"They didn't even tell me," he snapped. "I overhead them arguing one night. Apparently, Mom wouldn't have even known if Cynthia hadn't brought the girl to her work and dropped the bomb on her. That's what caused their divorce. Dad was more than a cheating bastard. He's complete scum. Who has two lives? Two homes. Two families? And you, turning your back on us saying you were going to live with him. It was too much. It destroyed Mom."

"Then maybe someone should have told me. Why am I always guarded? You all treat me like I'm some innocent child, but what do you expect? I know nothing! Jesus. This stupid cabin thing—Dad. What the hell is next?"

"Boston. But you can't tell me I didn't warn you about that because I did."

"Don't start with me. Boston is the only one who's been honest."

"You're wrong, Luce."

Jeff hooked his arm in mine, leading me in a different direction, and I didn't argue. I didn't even speak. More snaps of wood sounded as time went on and on. Ignoring them was easy while I weighed Jeff's newest confession. It took the prominent role and brought me back to my childhood. I let it play out, seeing my father—his smile, his appearance, his wandering eye. Even as young as I was, I didn't miss the way he stared at other women.

"Shit. I don't believe it. Lucy, look."

His aghast tone brought my head up. The back of a small wooden cabin rested far ahead, barely visible in the beam. Its rundown appearance sent chills down my spine. Jeff tried to pull me forward, but my feet wouldn't move. If this place really existed, what else about that day was true?

Chapter 11
Boston

One hour. Two.
One plan foiled. Then another.
The scene with Jeff and Lucy replayed in my mind. I let my anger fester, building as I stared at my reflection in my rearview mirror. For the life of me, I couldn't remember where my cabin was located. I saw it in my mind, but as for its whereabouts, I didn't have a clue. I cursed myself for not following when I could have, although something told me I wouldn't have made it far with my car. The terrain wasn't right. So how did I normally get there?

Three hours ticked by. I called my mother to see if she'd give me the location, but she didn't answer.

Darkness filled the interior, only illuminating when lightning flashed around me. The small town was relatively slow considering it was dinner rush, and from where I parked on the side of the old diner, I knew it wouldn't be long before it died down completely.

I picked up my phone for the hundredth time, clicking the button that said *SecureOne*. My empty driveway popped up on the screen and the heat within intensified. One by one, I swept my finger over, viewing the main quarters of my parents' home before flipping through the guesthouse. Nothing. No Lucy.

Tossing it back on the seat, my gaze shot to her road as thunder seemed to shake the car. I couldn't see her house from here, but I'd noticed before it was a dead end. If Jeff turned on their street, he would have to pass me.

More time. Endless seconds.

Aching throbbed in my jaw while my fingers white-knuckled the steering wheel. Each person who came into view suddenly became a target for my aggression. The thickening pressure within had my heart slamming into my chest. Lucy's face came in so clear as she told me I couldn't go. She'd stood up to me. She had emotionally pushed me away for her family—a brother I had spent my entire life protecting her from.

Another person passed. Another victim. Victim. Blood. Knives.

Colors strobed—red, almost black—pale skin. A man. Lightly marbled meat.

I blinked the fuzzy images away, slamming the side of my fist against the steering wheel as hard as I could. Picking up my phone, I hit the security, roaring and hitting the wheel once more when our place remained empty.

Where the hell were they? Did they find anything? Were the cops looking for me this very second? No…they'd be at my house. My mother wasn't even there. My dad was in the city, and she'd decided to meet him for the weekend. He had always worked a lot. I wasn't even sure I knew him before the accident.

More time.

As if the universe felt how close I was to combusting, a woman stopped at the end of the building to watch for cars so she could cross. I knew who it was from her small size and dampening blonde hair. And she was alone. It was late. Most of the cars were gone, only a handful remaining throughout town. I let her cross the street and waited a good twenty minutes so she could make it home and settle in. When I turned on my car and drove across the street to their road, most of the neighbors' lights were off.

I pulled into the driveway, heading to the front door. Two knocks, and she eased open the barrier. "Boston?" Her head moved to the side as she tried to look around me. "Are you okay? Where's Lucy?"

"I don't know. I'm worried. Jeff came by and picked her up. He was really upset and managed to convince her to go searching through the woods for a cabin…" I paused, frowning. "The one we supposedly killed a girl at. I tried to tell them to wait until morning, but Lucy promised they wouldn't be long. That was hours ago. I don't know what to do. I thought maybe you could go with me to help search? I'd go by myself, but my memory isn't the best, and I'm afraid every time Jeff gets around me, he turns violent. Lucy doesn't need to see that."

Fear had her mouth opening and she quickly nodded. "Please, come in. I'll change real quick."

The diner uniform she wore smelled of a mix between chicken fried steak and coffee. I wrinkled my nose, following her into the living room as she put down her wine glass. The moment her bedroom door closed, I pushed my hand into my pocket and tapped against the bottle of pills I'd taken from her medicine cabinet only hours before.

Within a few minutes, Lucy's mom was breaking from her room. She looked anxious, which was perfect.

"I was thinking, you should probably call the cops or something. I don't know where to begin. Lucy and Jeff could be anywhere. The more help we have, the better."

"Right. Yes." Her hand pressed against the side of her head. "I can run next door and ask the Olsons if I can use their phone."

"No need. I have mine."

I took out my cell and handed it over. The frantic tinge lacing her voice soaked into my calculating brain and I studied every little difference in her tone as she explained the situation. "Yes, please. My daughter's boyfriend said they've been missing for hours. My son, he's not mentally…well." She paused. "He's been seeing a doctor, but I'm not sure if he's been taking his medication. We're headed out to search now." She looked over at me. "Where do you think they went?"

I shrugged. "Maybe just outside town? Five to ten miles away? But I really don't know."

My response was relayed and she talked to them a little longer. When she hung up and handed the phone over, I smiled.

"Excellent. Before we leave..." I pulled out the medicine bottle and watched as her brow wrinkled in confusion. "You should probably take *your* pills."

"Wait...how did you get those?"

The back of the sofa was behind me and I leaned against it, twisting the top free. "I swiped them earlier while you were at work. You know, depression isn't always fixed with a prescription. Sometimes, there's nothing we can do to change what we feel." Little white pills spilled into my palm until it was empty. "Sometimes...we just can't cope with life anymore."

"Boston, what are you doing?"

She went to step around me, but I put myself in her path, shaking my head.

"Lucy needs me. Not you. Not Jeff. She loves me...and I *more* than love her. So, you're going to voluntarily take these, or I'm going to be forced to do something you won't like."

Fear grew and a broken breath shook her chest. "You did kill a girl, didn't you? He's not sick...J-Jeff's not lying."

Tears raced down her face as her hands searched behind her while she walked backward. I took the knife from my pocket, flipping the blade free with a flick of my wrist. She immediately jolted to a stop.

"Well...he could be...but I think he might be telling the truth. You see, I don't remember exactly what happened, but I have a very strong feeling maybe his words hold a little weight, *if you know what I mean*."

"Please, let me take my babies and leave. You never have to see us again. We'll never say anything."

"Take Lucy away from me? Not on your life. You're going to swallow these pills or we'll do this the fun way. We'll wait until Jeff gets home and I'll make him watch you suffer like you can't imagine. With Jeff so unhinged, who wouldn't believe he killed his mother? I mean, he's seeing a shrink, he's taken his sister on some hunt for a delusion only he believes. You just told the police how unwell he is. Why wouldn't he kill you, and then himself? It's perfect, really. Think about it. The neighbors have seen his outbursts. The authorities assume the worst. When they hear this story and Lucy corroborates his unstable behavior, it'll all fall into place. No one will bat an eyelash.

Green eyes widened and moved to stare at the ground as her mind raced.

"Your choice, Ms. Adams. Suicide or murdered by your beloved son. What do you want the world to know of your demise?" Her legs flexed, and I snapped my hand up to trace the blade along her cheek as she sobbed. "Before you decide to run or fight me, like you're about to, know if I hit you once—game over, bitch. You choose your son's fate. When you do, I will draw out every ounce of pain imaginable and prolong it until you *beg* me for death. Don't be a hero," I said, moving closer. "Lucy will take your suicide better than her brother killing her mother. Think about it. Do what's best for your children and swallow these fucking pills so we can get on the road."

Time dragged out while I waited for her to choose. She wasn't a real fighter. I knew it in my gut. Harder, she cried, finally lifting her hand.

"No. Open your mouth."

"Please, Boston. Don't do this. We can get you help."

"Lucy is all the help I need. *Open.*"

A strangle sound left her as she obeyed. Dumping a large amount into her mouth, I covered her lips with the side of my fist. "Swallow."

Shoulders caved and she was shaking almost convulsively as she tried to force them down. Once, twice, she swallowed. She seemed to gag before managing to get them down her throat.

"Open. Let me see."

When there was no evidence of any left, I poured in the remaining pills. A smile wanted to come, but I held it in, grabbing the full glass of wine. She chugged the dark liquid, sobbing even harder as her panicked eyes searched the room.

Survival instincts were kicking in, but she wouldn't outlive this. I wasn't going to let her.

"You've done the right thing. I'm going to take such good care of your daughter. You have my word."

"No. Lucy will know. She's smart."

I laughed, putting the glass down and grabbing her purse. "I'm smarter. Lucy will never suspect, and even if she does, I'll convince her otherwise. Your biggest mistake right now is underestimating how far I'll go to make sure she's mine."

More tears. More time. Finally, she swayed and blinked slowly.

"I do believe that's our cue. Time to go. You make a fucking sound and this blade goes through your side."

I wiped the empty bottle of pills and closed her fist around it before tossing it to her bedroom floor. Leading Ms. Adams to the car appeared like I was helping her more than anything. And I was. I kept her close, leaning not inches from her face as she tried to keep from falling to the side. Rain pounded against us and worry for Lucy had me nearly dumping her inside. When I slid into the driver's seat, her eyes were closed and she looked on the verge of getting sick. I strapped her in and eased her head back as her breaths quickened.

I reversed, taking my time through town. Anxiety riddled her broken breaths and my palm flattened over her forehead, pushing back as her head bobbed.

"You just lie there and close your eyes. Think of happy times."

"You're...not going to..." A dry heave sent her forward, and I slammed her back into the seat. "Luc..." The slurred word died off as her eyes rolled and then closed. Light from the town disappeared and trees lined on our sides. I took the turns, winding us deeper into the darkness. Within minutes, vomit trickled from her mouth as her body convulsed violently next to me. Gurgling played the loveliest duet of death. I did smile then. She was choking.

Asphyxiating next to me as she began to swipe her fingers down her throat.

I slowed at a dirt road, making sure no other vehicles were around. What started off as a relatively smooth path turned bumpy. My car slid through mud and scraped underneath from the large potholes. Farther, I went, purposely moving in the direction of a large rut. I eased through, jerking to a stop as the tires spun. Harder, I stepped on the gas, letting it get good and stuck.

Lucy's mom fell to the side, and I reached over, leaning the seat back and pressing my fingers to the pulse point at her neck. If there was a beat, it was faint. But I felt nothing.

Time.

Bright light from my high beams lit up the space. Stepping from the car, I turned it off and snagged the keys as I walked the surrounding tree-line.

"Lucy!"

I called out her name, repeatedly, loud and with purpose. My fear skyrocketed. Pulling out my phone, I hit redial. An operator came through, and my voice shook with true emotion.

"Hey, this is Boston Marks. I'm calling to check on the search going on for Lucy and Jeff Adams. I'm out here with their mother, but I don't see anyone. Are there people looking? Are we in different spots? My car is stuck and I can't make it back to the main road."

"Mr. Marks, do you know your location?"

"No. The road wasn't marked. I'm maybe ten miles north of town."

A pause. "I'll call and inform them. We'll see if we can find your location."

"Great. I'll be out calling for Lucy. Maybe if they're close they'll hear me."

Hanging up, I pulled security again. Nothing. My teeth ground together and anger flourished. Heading back to the car, I opened my door, leaning in. Water dripped from my hair, splashing against the leather. The smell of bile had me holding my breath. Lucy's mom's skin was so white, it didn't look real. I stared, fascinated, at her slightly open eyes and parted mouth. She was staring toward the ceiling and there was white residue mixed in with vomit on her lip. The substance was soaked into the top of her light pink shirt. Dead. She was definitely dead.

Lucy. This was for the best.

I stood, heading back to the trees.

"*Lucy!*"

An hour later, maybe less, lights flooded down the road. I kept yelling, only backtracking toward my car as a big truck stopped directly behind where I was stuck. Two men got out, and I called out once more as I waved to them, jogging back in their direction.

"Any luck? Have you found Lucy or Jeff?"

A short, stocky man walked up next to a taller, gray-haired man. They were both wearing uniforms.

"Not yet. Volunteers are pouring in. We'll find them soon, son. Can you tell us what happened?"

I took a deep breath. "Jeff, Lucy's brother, came by our house earlier. We're living in my parents' guesthouse. He's been…" I paused, glancing toward the car, then dropped my voice, appearing as if I wanted to guard Ms. Adams from hearing. "We used to be best friends. Ever since the accident where he hit me in the head with an axe, he's been having these weird breakdowns. I think he blames himself for almost killing me."

"We know the story," the shorter officer said. "I was on scene when we took you to the hospital."

My eyes widened. "Then you know. Well, since I've been awake, he's invented this story about some cabin in the woods and a body." I sighed. "We were making a horror movie there right before the accident. Somehow, I think he's convinced himself the entire thing was real. He came over begging Lucy to go with him so he could prove to her these delusions were real. She didn't want to go, but he started getting threatening and erratic. More toward me, not her. I tried to make her stay, but she wanted to try to show him what he believed wasn't real. So, she went in an attempt to calm him down. That was hours ago. I'm sick with worry something's happened."

"He was in the station not long ago for attacking you at the hospital. You didn't press charges."

I shook my head. "I don't blame him for what happened. I was stupid for getting so close. I just wish he wouldn't blame himself. We're all taking it hard. I still don't remember my past. My best friend scares me now. Hell, *he scares us all*, but I can't imagine what he went through during the time I was in a coma."

"We'll get it straightened out when we find them. Did you tell dispatch Ms. Adams is with you?"

"Yes. She's in the car. She wasn't feeling very well when I picked her up. I think she was crying," I said lowly, glancing back toward the passenger side again. "She's hasn't looked very good lately. I told her to rest, that I'd search. She could barely walk when we left the house. I'm not sure whether it was the wine she was drinking or she's getting the flu. I'll let her know you're here. I'm sure that'll put her at ease."

I headed in the direction, opening the door as they followed.

"Ms. Adams?" My head reared back at the smell and I cocked it to the side, shaking her shoulder as her deathly pale face rolled at the movement. More liquid dribbled from her mouth, streaming from her chin. "M-Ms. Adams, are you okay?"

Urgency, fear, confusion. They thickened my tone as I shook her once again and surged back. I nearly plowed over the smaller officer, hitting the ground hard as I scrambled away.

"She's…is she…?" Somehow, I gagged, digging my fingers into the mud as I dry heaved.

"Oh, hell." The older officer crinkled his nose, whispering to the other before moving in to talk on his radio.

"What's wrong with her? Is she...? She's not fucking...dead...right?"

"Son, just calm down. We have an ambulance on the way."

I gagged again. Surprise had pride swelling, but I was more interested in the sympathy lighting the officers' faces as I tried to catch my breath. Their concern over me was genuine. It was real. This was going to work, and if Jeff was smart, he'd kill himself before I had to do it for him.

Chapter 12
Lucy

My lips pressed together tightly as I glared at Jeff. It took all my strength to walk through the broken door of the cabin. I was afraid. Terrified at what I'd see. But I hadn't expected this. Or maybe I had. Perhaps that was why I was so mad. When the cabin first came into view, I almost believed him. But it was all lies.

"What now?"

His head shook as he shone the flashlight around the empty bedroom for the millionth time. We had searched the entire place up and down. Nothing. No blood. No torture devices or a single knife. "I don't understand. This place was packed with things. Furniture. Pictures. Equipment and shit. It's gone. Everything is gone."

"Probably because it never existed! Jeff, it didn't happen! None of it. None!"

My entire body shook from the fury and cold. I was drenched from the rain, and it was freezing. We'd walked so far, for what? Nothing. Jeff was still in denial, and my legs ached so bad, they were barely able to support me. Exhaustion became crippling, and all I wanted to do was to get back to Boston. He was probably worried sick.

"I want to go home, *right now*. If I ever hear you mention anything about this again, I'll never speak to you again."

Without waiting for him to follow, I stomped to the front door, not even worried about the dark. A hand gripped onto my shoulder, spinning me as rain pattered back over my head. Thunder boomed in the distance, and I swatted his hand off me.

"Lucy, don't be mad. There's a cabin. See, I told you there was. I'm telling the truth."

"No, you're not. There's a fucking cabin. So what? Have you seen Boston's house? I'm not surprised. They have money. Maybe it's his dad's hunting cabin. You both used to go hunting when you were younger. It means nothing."

I kept walking as Jeff jogged to make it to my side. "Dammit, Lucy. I swear—"

"What did I tell you? Not another word, Jeff, or you and I are done. You need help. Mom has enough on her plate. She doesn't need this. She's barely keeping it together as it is. First Dad, then your accident with Boston, then the drinking episodes, and now…you're turning into a raving maniac. People are talking. Sarah asks about you all the time. When was the last time you talked to her? When's the last time you went to work? Have you even been helping Mom out with the bills?"

"You're one to talk. You left."

"I could barely contribute with what I made. Besides, I was on my way to work tonight, but *you* convinced me to come on this stupid trip. *So stupid*. No more. I'm finished worrying about you. I just want to be with Boston, and I want to be happy."

Again, I was grabbed. I screamed, swinging at him as I fought to break loose.

"You can't go back to him, Lucy. Don't you see how dangerous he is? We need to get Mom and leave. Or…I'll kill him this time. Then we'll never have to worry about him getting to you."

"Do you hear yourself? You're the dangerous one! Let go!"

I clawed at his face, kicking out and hitting against him the best I could. When I managed to break free, I took off running into the darkness. Branches scraped my face, tearing into my skin worse than before. The flashlight swayed within the higher branches before me, and I cut between trees, putting my hands out as I pushed myself impossibly faster. The jarring impact of a tree had air

exploding from my lungs. I crumbled, crying out from the pain.
Light.
"Lucy! Are you okay?"
"Stay away from me, Jeff!"
Warmth ran from my nose and I wiped the blood with my sleeve as I hobbled to stand. My ankle would barely support my weight. Jeff was breathing hard. Staring at my brother, I didn't feel safe. The look he held—betrayal, something courting psychotic—I didn't even recognize this person. He watched me like a predator. My mind scrambled over what to do. Staying quiet, he waited until there was distance between us before following. I was limping along, but I couldn't go fast. It made me even more nervous.

I glanced over my shoulder, trying my best to stay alert of his location. Tears broke free as the weight of the entire situation settled in at once. For the last few months, I couldn't remember the last time I could just breathe without worrying about something.

"Maybe you're right. Maybe…I do need help."
"You do."
"Especially for what I'm about to do."
A whimper left me, and I reached out to a nearby tree. "What?"
Footsteps approached, and I glared, looking back, but the expression quickly vanished as movement blurred toward me. Pain exploded on the side of my head and my legs buckled. I was falling, but not. Sound wavered, bringing Jeff's voice in and out.

"I'm sorry, Luce. This is the only way. I have to keep you safe."

****

Deep breaths.
My body was bouncing and jolting this way and that. Opening my eyes was torture, but the jarring was worse. I

cried out, vomit burning my throat as I fought the urge to be sick.

"*Jeff! Lucy!*"

Shouts in the distance broke through and I realized Jeff was running…running away from them. The awareness brought my body to life and I tried to fly up. My legs and arms thrashed, and Jeff stumbled as he tried to gain control of me.

"Stop," he growled out. "They can't find us. You have to be quiet."

"Help! Hel—"

My face was slammed into his shoulder as he tried to silence me. I fought harder, letting out a piercing scream while I began to swing. Dogs barked, growing closer. I let their deep sound drive me to wrestle harder. He was slowing, trying to block my hits.

"Enough, Lucy! You're going to get us caught. Then we will never be safe."

"We are safe. Let me down! If you want to run, run, but not with me."

Jeff's face was barely visible in the dark. The rain had finally stopped and the moon was the only thing casting a glow. He slowed to a stop, looking around panicked. "They're going to catch us like this. I'll come back for you."

"No, you won't. I'm not leaving anywhere. I never want to see you again. I can't believe what you've done."

The sob hurt worse than every word I forced out. My head felt like it was splitting in two. I was on the verge of throwing up and I was still so cold.

"You don't mean that. You're my sister."

"Not anymore. Look at me, Jeff. Look what you're doing right now."

Multiple beams of light cut through the trees and Jeff shifted on his feet, nearly dropping me to the ground.

"I'm sorry for your head, but you wouldn't have left otherwise. I'm coming back for you, Lucy. I hope it won't be too late by then."

Jeff took off racing into the darkness. The men were getting closer, and I was crying so hard, I could barely call out to them. The night didn't seem real. As Boston raced for me, it turned even more surreal.

"Lucy. God. Shit. Lucy, are you okay? What happened?"

People crowded around, and dogs howled and barked not far from me. Boston winced as he pushed back my hair, looking angrier than ever.

"Jeff...he's lost it." I sobbed, letting him pull me into his arms. "There was nothing in the cabin. Nothing, and he flipped out. He said we should kill you. He kept grabbing me and I tried to fight him and run away, but he hit me with the flashlight."

"Which way did he go?"

Raising my shaky hand, I pointed for the cop. "That way."

"Is he armed, ma'am?"

"What? No. I don't think so."

"Men!' The officer motioned, and a group gathered.

The trip back came in a blur of voices and more trees. Boston carried me the entire way, moving in next to me after they put me in the ambulance. It hadn't registered at first, but once it did, I began to try to climb out.

"I'm fine. I don't want to go. It's just a concussion and sprained ankle. Really, I just want to go home."

"Ma'am, we really think you should at least get checked out."

"No. I don't want to go. I'm okay."

Boston looked between the us, nodding to them. "I'll keep a close eye on her."

"Where's my mom? I need to see my mom. Is she here?"

He paused in helping me out. "Lucy, we need to talk."

"Later. My mom needs to know what's happened. God, she going to freak out about Jeff. I think he's gotten worse. He's lost his mind over this."

My palm pushed between my eyes at the throbbing. Voices were everywhere, increasing the excruciating sensation. Crunching from footsteps approached and two officers came into view.

"Lucy."

At my name, I nodded. "Officer…Jenson, right? We've met before."

"That's right." He paused, appearing grim as he shifted. "I'm afraid I have some bad news concerning your mother."

"My mom?"

"Can we do this later?" Boston asked quietly.

"Do what? What's wrong with my mom? Is she okay?"

From their expression, my mind wouldn't process what it could mean. Boston quickly turned me to him.

"When you didn't come home, I went to your mom's. I wasn't sure where else to go or what to do to find you and Jeff. I immediately noticed she was pretty upset, but…" Boston paused. "We called for help so we could search, and *we were* searching. She said she wasn't feeling well and went back to sit in my car while I did the walking."

My head whipped around, trying to find Boston's car. "I don't see it. Where did you park?"

"Lucy," the officer said, moving in. "I'm sorry. Your mom…she didn't make it."

"Didn't make it? Didn't make what? Make it here?"

"She passed, Lucy."

The hard shake of my head left my brain rattling. It didn't make sense.

"I'm so sorry."

"No. No," I yelled at the officer as they backed away. My fingers clawed toward Boston and I was crying again, falling down some endless hole where nothing would process. "He's mistaken. He—"

"No. I'm sorry, baby. I saw her myself. Me and the officers went to check on her…and she was gone." Moments turned hazy as he practically held me up. "They think maybe she took too many pills or something before I got there. She looked like she had been crying. They could be right."

"W-What? No. *My mom wouldn't do that.*"

"I'm sorry. I really am."

Boston hugged me tighter, leading us toward more people. I wanted to fight, to go crazy at the news, but I didn't have the strength. They talked, but I heard nothing. The ride from an officer consisted of me sobbing the entire way home. Even through Boston bathing me, I drifted in a fog of severe disbelief and guilt. When he finally put me in our bed and held me, I decided I'd be okay with never leaving this spot again. I didn't want to see how this part of my life was going to play out. Would they lock Jeff up for good in some mental hospital, or would he go to jail? Would I really have to plan a funeral for my mom? Nothing came, and I didn't push it. I held Boston tighter, wishing I'd wake up and this would just be another nightmare.

Chapter 13
Boston

Had I wanted Lucy to need only me? Yes. And I was thriving and eating up every moment I could help her. Almost two weeks had passed since I'd turned the tables in our lives. We buried her mother. Jeff was still on the loose. And Lucy...

"Sit, baby. You need to eat."

She was buried under the blankets, and it was already noon. All she wanted to do was sleep. Sitting for hours and watching her, I told myself she needed to adjust. She needed time to mourn. I wasn't too impatient. Only when she slept for long periods of time. *Like now*. But she would obey when I told her to wake, and that made it okay.

"I'm tired."

"You're hungry. Up. Come on."

A groan left her, and she sat. Tangled blonde hair covered her face and I reached up, rubbing it back as she remained sitting there with her eyes closed. Moments went by. Silence. Finally, she cracked her lids. They were red-rimmed and swollen from the bad dreams that kept her awake most of the night. Another pleasure I liked to take advantage of. I knew one way to calm her down, even though sometimes she tried to fight me when I touched her. If I didn't know better, I'd guess she liked the fight. It was the thing that got her the wettest, and at that point, I couldn't keep my hands off her. I liked the fight more.

"That's my girl. Open."

Lucy's lips parted as I brought the beef stew to her mouth. They twisted, and she shook head as she forced herself to swallow.

"You don't like it?"

"You can't eat stew cold, Boston. You have to warm it up."

"I did warm it up." I pushed my finger into the center of a carrot, throwing a glare at the microwave before I frowned. "I'll heat it up longer."

"Don't bother. I'm not hungry."

"You're going to eat."

"But I don't want to."

At my silent stare, tears collected.

"Uh-uh. What did we talk about? No crying."

"She wanted me to stay." A sob. "Boston, she wanted me to stay home. What if—"

"We talked about this too." I pulled Lucy onto my lap, rocking her. "What happened wasn't your fault. Your mom was probably just tired and overwhelmed with everything going on. She was on medication. Maybe it just wasn't enough."

"But w-why? Why didn't she come to me? Why didn't she t-try to talk to me so I could help? If I would have thought...God, w-why didn't I see it? I should have known she was so far gone, right? I mean...she was always tired. And she'd go to her room right after dinner. Why didn't I suspect something was about to h-happen?"

"I don't think any of us could have guessed how things turned out. I know you miss your mom. I know you're hurting, but you have *me*. I love you. I love you more than anything in this world."

"I know you do. I love you too." She nuzzled into my neck, growing quiet through the gentle sway. Despite the episode, she was getting better. They weren't lasting as long, and in a few more weeks, we could move on to our new normal—to our life together.

Grabbing the blanket, I carried her to the sofa while I headed back to warm up her stew. Lucy watched, but sat quietly.

"I was thinking maybe we could get out today. We need food, and a walk through the grocery store would do you good. Are you up for it?"

Her attention went down while she fumbled with her fingers. "I don't know. I really don't want to."

"But you know you need to, right?"

"Yeah."

"Good. Then after you eat, we'll get you cleaned up."

"Boston...we need to talk."

"About what?"

Lucy's eyes peeked up, but she lowered them again. "About lots of things. What are we doing?"

Beeping from the microwave sounded and I popped open the door, sliding the pot holder under the warm glass.

"We're going day to day. We're living. I'm not sure what you mean."

"I mean with our lives. What are we doing? I'm sure Sarah would take me back at the theater, but I don't want to work there for the rest of my life. My mom...she said something to me before I left. She didn't want me to stop living my life because you and I got together. She didn't want me to quit work or...grow up too fast, I think."

"So, you're referring to work, like jobs."

"Well, yes. Sort of. I mean, everything in general. You go to school...or will be returning at some point. I have to figure out what I'm going to do."

I carried the bowl over, contemplating her question as I handed it over.

"Go to school then."

"It's not that easy. I barely graduated from high school. I don't have the sort of money your family does. I mean, maybe I can get some loans while I go to the community college, but...I don't even know what I want to do. Why didn't I take this seriously before? Why didn't I listen to my mother when she talked about this a year ago?"

A sigh left me as I sat on the edge next to her legs. "You're thinking too much. There's no rush to do anything. I can't even start up until next semester, and you have plenty of time to decide what you want."

"I guess. But what will you do when the time comes?"

I got quiet, thinking it over. From what my mom told me, I drove the two hours to school daily. I knew this had to do with Lucy. But now that I had her...

"How would you feel about moving to the city?"

"The city?"

"Why not?"

"For one, it's expensive. For two...it's..." More tears collected in her eyes. "It's so far from home."

"But I'm your home now." I grabbed her hands, preventing her from continuing to mess with them. "I'm your home. Let's get a place together. Let's go to school together. You talk about money, but don't. That's all on me. I just want you. Let's make this work. We'll leave this place and never look back."

Silence.

"Think about it, baby. Give it time to soak in. You have to admit, there's not much going on for you in this town. And there's nothing wrong with a fresh start. I think we could both use one."

"You're right. Boston is far, but finding a good job will be easier, and going to school is a must."

"Yes."

Again, she was on the verge of crying. "What about Jeff?"

Anger ignited at his name. My jaw flexed, but I stayed calm. "What about him? *He hurt you.* Jeff needs help. Hopefully, they find him and he can get better. As for you, I don't want him anywhere near you again."

Wetness escaped and she wiped the tears as fast as they fell. She didn't respond, but she didn't have to. She wasn't stupid. To be near Jeff would result in her getting hurt, and she knew it.

****

"How long are they going to follow us around?"

A smile came as I examined a jar of olives and placed them in the cart. "I don't know. Maybe until they find Jeff? This is a small town. It's not like they have anything else to do."

"True. It's just weird always seeing a cop car in the distance." Lucy pointed to the spaghetti, and I tossed it in, kissing her as I moved to her side. Pride soared. Happiness flowed. Cops be damned, I was on cloud nine. I was always aware they were there, but I didn't mind. Let Jeff try to come back for what was mine. I wasn't unprepared. With the alarm always set at the guesthouse, I'd know if he tried to get in. And if he did, he'd regret it.

We walked farther, coming to a stop as Lucy scanned over the tomato sauces. Two kids raced by—a dark-haired boy and a young girl. The aisle rippled, changing as memories came flooding back.

"Take her with you, Jeff. Make sure you keep an eye on her, Jeff. Lucy, Lucy, Lucy. I'm so sick of Lucy." Jeff held a hand basket, throwing in a loaf of bread and glaring back at his sister. Her head was slightly lower, and I got the impression she was around five years old. Her tiny frame stood away from us, but close enough so she wasn't afraid. Jeff was being mean to her like he always was. I knew this as a wealth of knowledge returned. I could see within my memories, and the most defining one was the day I first saw her. They were the only two in the park. He was running around playing with some sort of action figure under a tree that had pink flowers, and she was standing amongst the fallen, looking so sweet as she smiled and pointed at the swings. Each step became harder as I glanced at the girl. Out of nowhere, he pushed her. My feet planted—shock hit…rage. A flicker of other memories barreled through on top of it. Other scenes of him somehow hurting her. Bully, bully, bully. Yes, he was that. It was the exact reason I befriended him. Not for him—for her.

"Ugh! Hurry up, Lucy."

We were back in the grocery store. He walked faster, and so did I. I kept a pace behind him, just in case I needed to protect her from his constant abuse. With his mom working so much and his dad never home, Lucy was our responsibility. Ours—not just his.

We got in line, and I glanced behind me just as Jeff crushed his foot on top of her shiny black dress shoe. A small cry escaped, and her head went down lower as her shoulders curled in and shook. She was crying, and my all too well known hate for him grew as I reached for a sucker and crouched. When green eyes rose, her lip trembled. She had no interest in the sucker. Just me as she searched my depths.

"I want one too."

Jeff's whiny voice beckoned me to slam my fist into his mouth, but I reached up and grabbed another sucker instead, handing them over to him. He smiled, tossing them in the basket as he reached for a tabloid just short of the conveyor belt.

Slowly, I leaned in, keeping my voice down. She watched me, inquisitive for such a small child. Intrigued. *"Don't cry, Little Lucy. You're too pretty to cry."*

"Boston?"

"Hmmm?"

Lucy's hand was on my bicep, and it took me a moment to collect my thoughts.

"You remembered something, didn't you?"

A smile came, and I couldn't stop myself from pulling her into my arms. "I did. We were here. Me, you, and Jeff. You were so small. You had on a white and blue flowered dress with the frilly socks you used to love. And those shiny black shoes. Do you remember them? I think you wore them every day for a year. One day, you didn't fit in them anymore and you cried. I remember that," I breathed out, laughing.

"I do too." She smiled. "Do you remember anything else?"

I went to speak, but gave a sad shake of my head. "No. Just little things like that. Even so little, you were beautiful. *Cute*."

"You were the cute one. You were always there, watching over me. Sneaking me treats. For a while anyway. Then Jeff caught on and he wasn't too happy about it."

"Really? I don't remember that."

Lie. She didn't have to know. If things turned out like I secretly hoped they would, Lucy didn't need any suspicions on my account. Let her think the best. She didn't need to know the worst.

"What else do we need?"

We turned down the next aisle and I glanced over the canned goods. "Well, how much house do you want to play? Right now, we're at semi-serious. We have spaghetti and frozen pizzas. Are we talking three to four courses, because if that's the case, I'd say things are getting into the super-serious category."

"We did talk about moving to the city together, and I already live with you now. Any more serious and you'll be carting me to Vegas. Let's settle for two courses and frozen food. I'm more of a traditional girl myself."

"And that's why I love you. Pizza one night. Spaghetti and garlic bread the next. We'll skip the salad, I guess."

Lucy laughed, and that's all it took for my soul to flourish. I couldn't deny there was a twinge of wanting to claim her completely. To make her mine in not only my eyes, but in the eyes of the world. Someday...

"This one," I said, pointing as we began to pass another aisle. "We need movie food."

We turned down the snack aisle—chips, nuts, and cookies. Lucy bit her lip like a kid in a candy store, but it vanished just as fast.

"*No*." My head shook. "You're thinking you shouldn't be happy."

"I shouldn't. It's too soon."

"Your mother would have wanted this. *She wanted this*, Lucy. Look at me." I angled her face back toward me. "On our way to look for you, she and I talked. I told her how much you meant to me. How I loved you, and how I would do anything, *and I mean anything*, to keep you happy. She wanted nothing more. I didn't understand it then, but she asked me to give you the best life I could, and I will honor her request for the rest of my days. So, smile, baby. Love every moment, because I do, and looking down on us, she'll love what she sees too."

Lucy's arms flew around my neck, but a young woman coming toward us had the store fading away again.

"What's the matter, Jeff? You don't want to knock this one around? Maybe because she's not Lucy. Here, let me." Screams echoed through the small cabin room. A blonde was tied to the bed, bloody and cut up. Jeff was fucking her...and crying as he did. I gripped the knife, switching hands as my arm drew back. Bone crunched under her cheek from my fist. I reared back, moving to her nose as I flattened the bone from the endless hatred surging within.

"Hit her! Hit her like you hit Lucy! Do it!"

Pushing the blade into the side of his neck, I watched the skin split as I dragged the sharp edge an inch in length.

"B-Boston. Please, man. What the fuck! I don't want to do this anymore."

His sobs came harder as I let him see the real me. The monster I had kept locked away all these years. I meant to teach him a final lesson before I killed him. To humiliate and torture him with grotesque, evil acts he was too cowardly to commit. *Him*—not me.

"Hit. Her. Hit her!"

Muffled, unrecognizable pleas poured from the girl's mouth—a girl I'd lured here just for him. She was from the city. From my school, although I didn't pick her up there. It was in the park where there were no cameras nearby. We had never talked before that day, and the conversation was brief. She either wanted to go with me to make the movie right then and there, or I'd choose someone else. She had no time to debate or run her mouth to anyone. It was perfect.

"Come on, you fucking pussy." I gripped his short blond hair, jerking back. *"Show me the kind of man you really are. Hit her!"*

I let go, and Jeff's fist connected with her mouth. It was nothing, barely a hit at all. I laughed, and he reared back, connecting harder. Then, almost full force. He was crying so hard, he could barely breathe, whimpering while tears and snot dripped and mixed with the blood draining from her face. She was unconscious again. And I was only getting started.

"Boston!"

A gasp exploded from my mouth and pain nearly crippled me. My pulse hammered, every beat echoing in my head. The light blinded me and warmth ran from my nose.

"Oh my God. Oh God. Hold on." Lucy dug in her purse, grabbing out some tissue and pushing it to my nose.

I could feel how wide my eyes were. How wild they were as I looked around jerkily, holding the basket so I wouldn't fall to the floor completely.

"Talk to me. Come on, look at me."

Green eyes leveled with mine, and I cupped the back of her head, pulling her forehead to rest against mine as I pushed myself to stand all the way.

"I'm okay."

"Did you remember more? I tried talking to you, but you were gone. You didn't even react when I shook you."

"Yeah. Fuck, my head. I have the worst migraine."

We turned, and Lucy held me. "We're leaving. We're done." She let go of the basket, but we were already in line. "Should I call an ambulance?"

"No, no. Don't do that. I just need to rest. Shit," I groaned, closing my eyes.

Each noise stabbed my brain. Wheels from the carts squeaked and rattled. There was loud talking and laughter coming from not far away. Even though I wasn't near the cleaning supplies, the smell made it to me, and my stomach roiled with the urge to throw up. Everything collided and my eyes snapped closed at the powerful light.

"You might have to drive us home. I don't think I can."

"Okay. Let's just go. They can put the food away."

I pulled her into my chest, hugging while I kept my eyes closed. Her concern—her love—meant everything. "This won't take long. We need the food. Here." My wallet rested in my back pocket, and I pulled it out with the key, handing them both to her. "I'm going to try to make it to the truck. Don't…don't talk to anyone you don't know. Actually, I think I'll stay."

"Don't be absurd, Boston. Go."

The nudge on my chest had my eyes cracking open and I nearly growled as I leaned in, kissing her. When I pulled back and headed to the entrance, each step was torture. Water pooled at the sunlight, and I swayed as I saw my second vehicle in the distance. I hardly ever drove the damn thing, and found it resting in my parents' garage.

Cabin. Yes…my truck. My special truck.

Chapter 14
Lucy

To say I was worried about Boston was an understatement. Three days the migraine lasted. By the time I finally got him to go in to the doctor, he could barely move. Vomiting, random nosebleeds, memories—they kept him in bed, in our now pitch black house. The medication was helping, but he couldn't stand to take it. The doctor said this was normal for what he'd been through, but I hated seeing him in so much pain. To make matters worse, he took me going back to work harder than I had hoped.

With the blackouts occurring more and more, driving me was out of the question. That left me taking the truck, leaving him at home. I half expected to walk in and have him curled in the covers. When I reset the alarm and went upstairs, I eased to a stop. He was sitting on the sofa with popcorn, watching a movie. Beer bottles were on the coffee table and I shook my head, surprised.

"Someone's feeling better, I see."

Boston jumped, spinning in my direction. He usually heard everything. Even the lightest sigh. But not this time, and the guilt on his face nearly stopped my heart. I didn't understand it, but I knew what I saw.

"Yes. Sorry, I was…" He quickly clicked off the TV and stood as he came over, kissing me. "How was work?"

"Fine." I pointed to the television. "What was that?"

He fidgeted. "Nothing. Just one of my films. It's no big deal. With school starting in a few weeks, I wanted to get caught up on projects I've made. Tell me about work."

"Can I watch it?"

"That?" Again, he shifted. "You don't want to see that. It's horrible."

Suspicion grew. His head lowered, and finally, through the silence, his eyes lifted to me.

"Lucy, you can't watch it."

"Why not?"

Silence.

"*Boston.*"

"You just can't, okay?"

I grabbed the remote from his hand, stomping around the sofa. Before I could click the button, he had me around the waist, spinning and pinning me to the black leather couch. The remote fell to the floor with a thud. Weight increased against my wrists, and his knees forced my thighs apart while he settled between them.

My thrash did little to deter him. Lips met mine brutally, and he let go of one of my hands to jerk up my uniformed shirt so he could squeeze my breast.

"I want to see what you were watching."

"And I want you to kiss me back."

"Then show me what you're hiding."

Boston's eyes narrowed. "I'm not hiding anything. And it's really not a movie, per say. It's more…a documentary."

"On what?"

More hesitation. When I didn't budge, he sighed. "You really want to see?"

"Well, hmmm…yeah, of course I do."

His features sharpened, not looking very happy. "Fine. One condition."

"What's that?"

"I get to have you while you watch."

"Fine."

My waist rocked as he tugged at the button of my black pants. I let him pull them off, and he bent, grabbing the remote and clicking the button. A circle of chairs rested in what looked like someone's living room. Men and women of different ages and ethnicities filled the seats. There was even a small child. A younger Boston had my pulse pounding even more. His hair was longer than it was now, but not by much.

"Hey, that's you."

He pulled my panties off, rubbing his finger from my entrance to my clit. He didn't speak, but I didn't expect him to. He was focused. Touching and getting me wetter as his digits rubbed over my folds.

"Now that we heard from Maria, let's move to the next. Perry, you're new. Do you want to tell everyone when you started having these disturbing thoughts?"

My head lifted, only stopping because of Boston's shoulder. He was kissing my neck. Sucking against it. Confusion swarmed, but I lay it back down, closing my eyes and listening as a finger slid inside me.

"I think I've always had them."

"Why don't we start at the beginning? Can you tell us the first memory you have where you knew maybe you weren't like everyone else?"

He paused. *"I guess I was four. It was late. I'm not sure how late. I can remember the hallway being so dark. I could barely see. There were sounds coming from my parents' bedroom. At the time, I knew it was my mother, but I wasn't sure what was wrong with her. I was afraid. I'm not sure how long I stood outside the door, but I finally got the courage to open it. When I did, I saw her...bouncing on someone. A man. He wasn't my father. They were kissing, and she was naked. The sight...I can't even remember walking to my father's gun cabinet. It was locked, but I was going to kill them. I wasn't afraid at that point. I wanted to. I wanted to so much, I cried when I couldn't get the large door open."*

"What is this?" My voice was breathless. Boston nibbled on my ear, sliding another finger in me as he pushed deep.

"A side of me you never knew." He lifted, looking at the screen, but stayed only inches from my face. Beer filled my senses, but I focused back on the screen as he spoke. "I hid my camera. No one knew I was recording. You see, these meetings were confidential. Secret. No judgment—no matter what you shared."

He grabbed the remote, hitting the fast-forward button until he came to a man appearing on the screen. The rubbing inside me continued, and he went back to sucking and biting against the junction of my shoulder as I gasped. I knew that man!

"Jeff, would you like to contribute this week?"

"Jeff?" My eyes widened, and I shifted underneath him uncomfortably. Lust twisted with concern—fear.

"We never used our real names. Listen, Lucy."

"Sure. Why, not." Boston sat straighter, leaning forward to rest his forearms just above his knees. *"I stayed at my friend's house again last night. For those who don't know, it's not my friend I care for. Actually, I can't fucking stand him. His little sister is the reason I'm there. Her name is Lucy. The first time I saw her, she was five. I was always a private child. I never felt the need for friends or companionship. But there was something about this little girl. She was…beautiful. My mind says angel. That's how I viewed her. So innocent. So pure.*

"Her brother, he pushed her. I can remember stopping as if my feet were cemented to the ground. It's like the entire world froze in time as her tiny little body fell through the air. Just like the flowers in the tree above her. They fell. She fell. She was the first person I ever felt anything for. Hate, disgust, I knew those from the earliest times. Her…I loved her before she even connected with the ground.

"We were inseparable from that moment on. If I wasn't at school, I was at my friends—watching her, watching her, always watching. Waiting. Still, I wait. She's thirteen now. She grows, but I…" He swallowed hard, rubbing his hands together as if agitated. *"Waiting is the hardest. It's worse than death. She can't know how I feel. No one can. I shouldn't want to kiss her or touch her, but I'd be lying if I said didn't want to. Or that I hadn't. My*

heart...fuck, my heart hurts. To not confess my feelings when she notices me for more than I am...she wants me too. I can see it. Despite her age, she knows we're meant to be together. The way she looks at me, it increases that...fucking anger. If she were older, or I was younger..."

"Jeff, you mentioned staying there last night. Did you find your way into her room again?"

I wiggled under Boston, flattening my palm against his cheek as I pushed his head up so he had to look at me.

"Of course I did. That night. Every night I'm there. I watch her sleep. Sometimes, I ease into bed and just hold her. She's such a hard sleeper. She never even knows. Once, when I was holding her, she turned and wrapped her arm around me. I thought I was going to have a heart attack. It would have been the perfect death. Her smell...strawberries. Sweet, just like her."

"B-Boston?" My mouth stayed parted. Shock kept me from thinking. Thoughts wouldn't come. Nothing would as he moved toward my face at a leisurely pace and rubbed the tip of his nose against mine.

"It was always you, Lucy. I've told you that."

"But..."

"Shhh. Any questions you have, I won't have the answers to. It hasn't all come back yet. Just take that as proof. My loyalty has always been to you. Always. There's never been anyone else. There never will be." His lips pressed into mine, and mine parted even more as his fingers withdrew, only to begin thrusting again. With his other hand, he reached and turned off the television.

My heart thumped wildly. *Think. Think.* So many questions, but they were having a hard time getting through with the way he was touching me. How did I not wake up? How did I not see how strong his feelings were? What else didn't I know? No...what else did, or didn't, he know?

"Wait."

"I've been waiting for days. I've missed this. Just kiss me."

"*Boston.*"

I pushed against his shoulders, and he rose, a serious look on his face. "I told you not to watch. What do you want me to say? I don't know the guy on the tape. He doesn't seem like me. I don't even remember that day or really anything about those meetings except it was a private place where I could confess what was so hard for me to deal with. Like therapy. God, were you not listening, Lucy? Did you not see how hard it was for me?"

"No, I saw. You said you came to my room every night. You laid in my bed next to me." I crawled back to a sitting position, unable to withhold my question. "Did you ever…? I mean…you said…what did you mean you touched me? Like…taking advantage?"

Nothing registered on his face. Not a single emotion.

"Of course not."

"Are you lying to me? You said…"

"Well, I obviously don't remember much, but from what I do recall, no. I probably meant in general."

"You're lying," I whispered.

My brow drew in, and although I had no clue whether he was telling me the truth or not, I played on the fact that he might be truly hiding something.

"Lucy, I held you. I smelled your hair. I waited. *I fucking waited*!" I jumped, and he closed his eyes, taking a deep breath. "I knew better than to fuck up," he said, calmer. "Doing something stupid would have caused me to lose you. I can't lose you. I've waited my entire life for us to get to this point. I just want us to be happy." His arms came out toward me. "I'm sorry. I didn't mean to yell and scare you. Come sit with me. Let me hold you."

"I feel like I don't even know you."

"Join the club."

The frown he gave had me hesitantly crawling over. I was confused. I loved him. I had always loved him. Would I still if I had woken up to find him in my bed all those years ago? Would I have been afraid and told my mom so she could ban him from our house? Would the girl in me have falsely loved him more because he had chosen me even then? In some sick, twisted way, I didn't want to know the answer to that. It was wrong. All of it was on a level I couldn't even grasp. Boston said he loved me. Love wasn't always good. My mom loved my dad until the day she died. Maybe he was a big part of why she'd killed herself. Love was poisonous when paired with pain. It turned toxic. Into mad love. *Obsessive* love.

Chapter 15
Boston

  Showing her the video was a mistake. A monumental mistake. Inside, I seethed. What the fuck had I been thinking? That she would understand? That she would grasp how intense my love was? No, I wasn't thinking. I'd mixed my pain pills with alcohol and was lost in fascination at the video. So much so, I hadn't even heard her come in. Hell, I'd watched it three times, barely remembering the first two. I couldn't focus. But that couldn't happen again. Migraine be damned, I couldn't afford a mistake like this. Lucy wouldn't even look at me. Even without remembering our entire past, I could read her better than a book. She was thinking. Thinking about whether she should, or could, trust me. She thought I was crazy.
  That only meant one thing: I had to start over. Completely fucking over. I had to slow down on touching her. I had to force myself to back off and give her space. I had to have discipline and obey what I'd been taught by Dr. Patron. But could I?
  Just the thought was overwhelming. It absolutely massacred what and who I was. My heart said I couldn't pull back now that I had gotten so far. My calculating, manipulative brain said if I didn't, I'd lose her. And it was right.
  "You should probably jump in the shower. I can start dinner."
  "But we usually cook together."
  The surprised tinge in her tone made me want to smile, but she didn't need my love or kindness right now. She needed to feel guilty. To regret having whatever thoughts she harbored.
  "It's okay. I can handle it. You should go."

I stood, placing her down and walking into the kitchen. Normally, I would have soaked in any inch of skin I could view, but I didn't even raise my gaze as I collected the ingredients. For a good minute, she stood there, until finally, she snatched up her clothes and took off. A smile did come then, but it didn't stay. The shower started, and like bait, my feet wanted to take me closer. I wanted to see her when she didn't know I was looking. I wanted to watch.

Heat built and sweat collected as I jerked a knife free of the cutting block. Light reflected from the blade, and I was suddenly standing over the blonde girl. Her broken body was in the forest, sprawled out on the ground as Jeff positioned himself to attack me. And I was loving the game I was playing with him. Loving it so much, I'd never felt more invigorated in my life. I had been waiting and training for this moment. And it was imperative he experienced unimaginable terror before I ended his life. With making him rape and beat that girl, I had touched down on it, but making him think he stood a chance to escape only to show him how wrong he was…that was the icing on the cake.

A yell tore through the trees while he raced forward. Just as he got to me, I jumped out of the way, pushing my palm into the middle of his back so hard, he hit the ground with a jolting force. He wasn't even able to catch his breath before my boot plowed into his side and stomach.

Once.

Twice.

Three times.

I kicked as hard as I could, leaving him gasping and clawing into the dirt as he tried to move away. Lucy's name kept leaving my mouth. Feeding his fear. Letting him know she was mine.

"I brought your knife. You ready to finish this girl off?"

"F—uck. You."

Gasps sounded as he tried to stand. I got a quick two-step start before I connected and sent him sliding back through the dirt.

"Last chance. You can kill or join her. The choice is yours."

"You're going to kill me anyway."

I paused, cocking my head as he struggled to stand.

"Why would I kill you? You're my best friend."

"Because...because of this!"

I shrugged, walking closer to the girl. "Slit her throat. Once you do, this ends. We'll never speak of it again."

"You're lying."

"I don't lie, Jeff. You know that. Slit her throat or I will be forced to kill you."

He sobbed, standing. "Why are you doing this?

"Kill her, Jeff!"

I tossed him the knife, knowing this wasn't over. He scrambled for the weapon, charging at me. It was the biggest mistake he could have made. My hand swept under and drove up, grasping and crushing his throat as I slammed him back to the dirt—back to where he belonged. Once I did, I locked around his wrist that held the knife and got so close to his face, I could smell his sweat.

"You really don't learn. First, you'll be punished, then you'll end this. Once you do, it's over."

My fist begged to slam into his face, but I knew better. I stood, driving my foot back into his body. I wasn't sure how many times I kicked before veins protruded from Jeff's bright red, pained face. Spit shot out of his mouth at my last kick. He was trying to escape again, but not away—toward the girl.

Twice he fell as he tried to lift to his knees. Moments passed as he gained strength, but I was out of patience. I dragged him the rest of way, dropping him as I jerked the top half of the unconscious girl up by her hair.

"End this, motherfucker."

His hand was trembling as he lifted himself and the knife. Even though he could barely hold the weapon, he didn't hesitate. Blood waterfalled from her throat as the pressure increased, and I smiled, gripping his shoulder as he finished. He stumbled away, panting, staring at me horrified. Then, he ran away. And *I let him.*

Confusion. It hit me hard, bringing back the anger a million-fold. Why hadn't I killed him when I had the chance? Why had I let him escape? Was I fucking stupid?

I pulled out the carrots, chopping through them like I was feeding an army. When it wasn't enough, I took out the celery, then an onion, then potatoes. I had no idea what the hell I was going to do with it all. I moved everything over to a pot and filled it with water. My mother had bought healthy food, and I suddenly realized maybe I ate like this before. I had been a lot bigger than I was now. *A lot bigger.* And more powerful.

My head lowered, taking in my lean frame. I still had muscle and a six pack, but something told me that was genetic. It wasn't who I was or what I had worked so hard to become. Even my face looked different than my memories. And my scar...I tried not to look at it, but it wasn't going away.

"Boston? Are you okay?"

Lucy headed my way. Slow. Hesitant. She was already dressed, which tore at me even more. But she was wearing my t-shirt, so there was solace in that.

"Yeah. I just realized how different I look. I mean, I saw before, but I think my overall change is really starting to hit. You..." Fear, I didn't like it, but the emotion edged in as I thought over my worries. *Lucy, her opinion meant everything.* "The scar. Does this bother you? I know you were attracted to me before the accident, but are you less attracted to me now that I have it, or that I'm smaller? My muscles were a lot bigger. I can get like that for you again if you want. I can start tonight. Right now, while this is cooking."

"Whoa. Slow down." She came forward, glancing toward the stove. "You remembered more while I was gone."

Hesitation. I was drunk. I had to watch what I said. I was already babbling when I should have been standoffish.

"Just my lifestyle." My head shook, and I tried to tone down the anxiety concerning what her judgement meant to me. "Did you like me better that way?"

"Boston." A deep breath left her as she came forward and wrapped her arms around my waist. "I like you however you are. It was never about your looks. It was deeper than that."

My eyes closed and I rested my head on top of hers. "I think I'd like to start working out again. I felt better that way. And I could…" I was going to say protect her, but no, she couldn't see that part of me again so soon. I had to keep from being overbearing, no matter how hard it was.

"You could, what?"

"I could really focus on me. That's important. If we're going to have a life together, I need to be the best possible version of myself. You deserve that."

I gave her a quick kiss on her head and let go, putting distance between us. Before I heard the step forward, I felt her. Lucy's presence was a like a security blanket, comforting the beast. He always lurked, waiting. Waiting for what, I now knew. *Jeff. Men like Jeff. Jeff. Jeff.* Yes, I wanted him dead with a hunger I couldn't suddenly bear. Whatever happened before was my mistake, but it was time to fix that.

Chapter 16
Lucy

"Boston was two in this picture. We were living in the city at the time. In Boston—that's where he got his name. Gilbert and I met at a restaurant. I thought it was love at first sight. He was…handsome and powerful in his nice suit. He was surrounded by men dressed just like him, but he took one look at me and I knew my life would never be the same. I was young here, visiting relatives. Gilbert swept me off my feet. He stopped me just before I walked out the door and we've pretty much been together ever since."

Joy smiled, flipping to the next page of the photo album. "Boston was born less than a year later. Gilbert and I married when I was seven months pregnant. We stayed in the city for the first three years, then he moved us here. Such good times."

I mirrored her smile, sweeping over the memories that kept causing her to tear up.

"He's gone a lot now. Will I meet Boston's father soon?"

"Oh…" She glanced over. "Yes, I suppose he'll come home for Christmas. I guess it's time for him to meet you. I have to be honest, Lucy, I wasn't very accepting of this at first. I was worried for Boston, for both of you, but…you calm him. You make him better. I see that now. And you seem happy."

"I am. Thank you. What happened between Boston and his father?"

She paused, flipping to the next page. "The two of them don't get along very well. They haven't for years. It's nothing in particular, just little things that have happened and built over time."

"I see. Well…maybe now." I frowned as I turned my attention to the large glass windows that gave us a view of the guesthouse. Boston was probably still downstairs working out. That's all he ever seemed to do anymore. For the last week, he had lived in the gym. He hadn't even tried to touch me, which was so unlike him. I had been afraid before, but now I just...*needed him*. There were so many times I wanted to go see my mom. To ask her what to do, or just hear her voice. Even the need to talk to Jeff was there. Someone. Anyone. Now, I didn't even feel like I had Boston.

"We'll see how it plays out. Gilbert's supposed to call me after his meetings." She quickly shut the book, standing. "Boston mentioned heading into the city soon to get a new car. Maybe you both can meet him for lunch."

"I would love that. I'm sure Boston would too."

I rose from the sofa, following her to the door. She gave me a quick hug and I headed out as a car pulled into the driveway. My feet grew heavy and I came to a stop as an older man stepped out. At the sight of him, my pulse exploded. I'd seen him before. More than once. At the hospital, the day Boston woke up, and...the movie of Boston. The doctor. Yes, he was the man talking and asking the questions.

"Well now, what do we have here? You must be Lucy. Joy told me she had a new addition to her family."

Taken aback, I forced a large smile. "Yes, we met at the hospital. I'm sorry, I don't remember getting your name."

My hand went out, and he shook it. "Dr. Patron. I'm actually here for Boston. Is he around?"

"He's in the gym."

"Great. Before I talk to him, I'd like to ask you a few questions if that's okay."

"All right."

The older man's white hair blew back from the wind, and I took in his leather clad hands, fancy suit, and trench coat.

"I'm not sure if Boston's remembered or told you about me, but I'm his therapist. He's been seeing me since he was young. Twelve, to be exact. I know you've known him for just as long. He's always been a quiet boy. Very shy. Very reserved. Would you agree that was his behavior before the accident?"

"Yes."

"You're closest to him. Would you say that's his behavior now?"

I took a moment to think over his question. "Not toward me. Not anymore, but around other people, I'd say yes."

He nodded. "And how would you describe his emotional status? Is he happy most of the time? Angry? Does he upset rather easily?"

Unease settled and I looked toward the guesthouse. "Most of the time, he's great. There are moments he gets upset. I wouldn't say he gets overly mad." I paused. "I have noticed he doesn't like to be away from me. He'll pace. That's really it, though."

"Perfect." He glanced back toward where Boston was. "I heard your mother recently passed. How are you? Is Boston helping you with that?"

A slight smile wanted to come as I thought over just how supportive he'd been. "Boston is the only thing keeping me together right now. I don't know what I'd do without him. He's been amazing."

A grin appeared. "I'm happy to hear that. And he's in the gym, you say?"

"Yes, right this way." My hand gestured, and he followed as I opened the door and turned left. Boston was right where I knew he'd be. But he wasn't lifting weights like I'd thought. He had his earphones in and he was hanging from a bar doing pull-ups. His six-pack tightened through the fluid motion, and his muscles bulged in his arms. It had my eyes widening as I took him in. He already looked bigger after only a week.

As if he knew I was there, his lids rose, and he paused in the hanging motion before dropping to the ground.

He pulled the headphones out, not saying a word as he grabbed a towel to wipe the sweat from his face.

"Dr. Patron is here to see you. I'll just be outside."

"Outside?"

Boston headed in our direction, the concern visible in the way his speed increased.

"Yeah. I thought I'd take a walk around the property or something. Nowhere far. Just around."

"I can go with you if you want to wait. This won't take long."

I laughed, stepping back toward the main door. "It's okay, really. Take your time."

Before he could work harder to convince me, I headed back out the door. I wasn't sure what to think about the doctor being here. I had seen the type of patients he kept and heard where Boston fit in. It was all because of me. But now that he had me, what exactly did that mean?

The door shut behind me, and I turned toward the side of the guesthouse. The tree-line opened into a path and memories of Boston chasing me filtered through. But not for long. Movement had me jolting to a stop. Twigs snapped and I jumped as a squirrel raced up the tree.

Pushing my hands into my jacket pocket, I rolled my eyes, continuing. Deeper, I went, walking slowly through the slightly rolling terrain. Crunching. *Footsteps?* I walked faster while scanning my surroundings. The forest wasn't as dense here at it had been by the cabin, but it didn't ease the feeling of being watched.

Minutes went by and I rounded to the far side, knowing I was somewhere behind the main house. Darkness enclosed around. It had been overcast, but it almost appeared night as the trees encircled above. Rustling had me spinning just as a dirty hand slammed over my mouth. Mud was caked to Jeff's face and his eyes were bloodshot and wide as shuddering breaths shook his entire body.

"Shhh-shhh." He broke down, letting go and crushing his arms around me in a hug. "I didn't think you'd ever come. Tell me it's not true," he sobbed. "Tell me Mom's not dead."

The urge to fight was there, but at the mention of my mother, pain had it wavering. I held Jeff, letting my sorrow release for only a moment before I jerked free.

"It's true. They say she overdosed on pills. She...killed herself."

"She wouldn't do that. She wouldn't have left us." He cried harder, wiping his face as he tried to get close to me again. "This is my f-fault. He did it because of me. Because I tried to take you away."

"Boston didn't kill Mom," I snapped. "She took them before he even got there. Besides, do you hear how crazy you sound? You need help. This has gone too far. You have to turn yourself in. I won't press charges for what you did in the forest. Just get help, Jeff."

I turned, heading back the way I came. Distrust had me on my toes. Jeff lunged just like I feared he would, but I was ready. I sprinted with everything I had. A scream barely broke from my lips before he crashed into me. We slid through the dirt, fighting to get control of one another. My fist swung, but he deflected almost every hit.

"Don't do this, Lucy. All we have is each other. We have to hurry."

Fingers tore into my jacket as he attempted to lift me. I kicked against his thighs, screaming and clawing at his forearms. Pain tore into my hair as he used it to drag me off the path. The harder I fought, the rougher he jerked, grabbing more.

"Let. Go. Of her."

He stopped and let go at Boston's cold tone, raising his hands as he backed away. I rolled, seeing Boston standing not feet away with a shotgun. He had it at his side, glaring ahead. When I jerked back to Jeff, he was already gone. Not once did Boston look away from the darkness ahead as he came and helped me up.

"Are you all right?"

"You could have killed him."

Intense eyes lowered to me, but only for a second. "I could have, but would you have wanted me to?"

"N-No. Of course not." My arm wrapped around his. When he immediately pulled away, it left me feeling empty. He took a step, handing me the gun.

"I didn't think so. Take this and go back to the house. I'll look for him. Jeff has to be brought in. If I can find him, we'll call the cops and have him taken care of."

"You don't want me to call them now?"

"If I can't find him, they won't either. Let's spare alerting the police if we don't have to."

Boston began forward when I reached out, taking his hand. "I don't want you to go. What if something happens to you? I couldn't take that. I can't lose you."

Emotion drew in his features and his lips pressed in mine, full of heat—full of passion. My arm wrapped around his neck while I pulled him in closer.

"Stay with me. Go back inside with me," I begged.

"Don't ask me to do that. I can't bear telling you no. I'll be back soon. I love you." He kissed me harder, breaking away and running off through the trees at a surprising speed. Fear drove me back down the path at a jog. Just as I made it to the tree-line next to the guesthouse, I slowed to a stop. Mrs. Marks and Dr. Patron stood at the entrance, and Joy was shifting her feet nervously.

"We heard you scream." Her eyes went to the shotgun in my hand, then behind me. "Where's Boston?"

"He went after Jeff. I think he's going to try to convince him to turn himself in."

The two looked at each other, and Dr. Patron held her shoulder securely. Something unknown to me passed between them. It was enough to have Joy calming. His hand came out to me as he smiled. "Come, child. It's cold out here. Let's get you some hot cocoa. Boston will take care of this. After today's talk, I'm positive he'll get your brother all the help he needs."

Chapter 17
Boston

"Jeff...come on. Let's finish this. You know you want to."

Tracking Jeff wasn't easy. From what I could remember, we were both experienced hunters. But I had the edge. I knew these woods like the back of my hand. I didn't need all my memories to go where intuition led me. And it was in the right path. Footprints came at random. Some were fresh. *He was close.*

"Don't you want to talk about your mother? You missed the funeral."

I kept going, pushing myself faster as I weaved through the trees before checking more tracks. A good mile went by and a clear boot print had me cutting to the right. Two steps around a large tree and pain exploded across my face. Wood from the baseball-sized branch shattered at the impact, and I landed flat on my back. Air was impossible to take in, and pinpoint dots of light speckled my vision as he stepped up, looming above. Sweat streaked down the mud covering his dark face, and pants left his chest rising and falling.

"You killed my mother."

The kick to my stomach had the oxygen I'd just taken in leaving me.

Once.

Twice.

Three times, he kicked.

I groaned, rolling to the side and grabbing his foot, messing up his fourth attempt. He landed on his side while we both fought to get up faster than the other. Trickling of warmth streamed from my cheek toward my jaw, itching, distracting me as he threw his weight, tackling me back down.

His fist drew back, swinging for my face. The connection to my cheek was barely a graze. Laughter flowed from me as my need for this soared. I grabbed the side of his neck, controlling his movement as I pulled him toward my chest. Sticks stabbed and cut into my bare back while we rolled along the ground.

"Yeah, I killed your mom," I said, slamming my elbow into the back of his head. "I fucking shoved those pills down her throat while she cried and swallowed her shitty-ass life away. I did her a favor."

Jeff roared, wrestling my hands as he made it on top of me. Again, his fist slammed into my face. And I let him. The first hit was enough to stun. The following three only added to the foggy feeling, but my instincts reigned. I didn't know defeat. I knew to win. To get what I wanted. *To kill to keep what was mine.*

My foot pressed into the ground and I rolled us, taking my spot over him. Once I started hitting, I didn't stop. A tooth broke under my force. His cheek bone shattered.

"You should have seen her, Jeff. She was terrified. Crying. *Weak.* She didn't even put up much of a fight. She wanted to be rid of you."

A groan snuffed out the aggravated sound. His fight was ending. No matter how hard he tried to wiggle and break free, he couldn't remove me from my position. Puffiness rose around one of his eyes, swelling it shut. My arms were weak from working out, but I didn't care as I put everything into a hit that jolted his entire body. Jeff was barely conscious. His head lolled to the side and a sound got cut off as he choked on the blood filling his mouth.

"If we were back at the cabin, I'd scalp you for pulling Lucy's hair. God, I fucking want to. You thought what we did to that girl was bad. You should have seen what I've done. What I'm capable of. *Men.* Men like you. They never knew what was coming. I waited for this. For you."

Jeff coughed, spitting out blood from the deep tears in his lacerated lips. "Lucy. Lu—"

"Don't you dare say her name." I hit him again, keeping my hands in fists so I didn't tear out his tongue with my bare hands. "Why didn't I kill you after you slit that girl's neck? What happen when I went to your house?"

"Who...knows. You're...f-fucking crazy."

Despite the heaviness in my arms, I slammed my fist into his nose with each word. "What! Happened!"

A feeble yell echoed and he tried to roll and curl into himself, but he didn't have the strength.

"I...don't know. You showed up...with your camera. The movie stuff was already laid out from our filming...the day before." He paused, groaning and trying to catch his breath. "You stepped from around the house just as I was walking up. You were waiting. I ran right for...the axe."

Something wanted to come, but didn't. Did it even matter? I had Jeff here now. I had a..." My eyes shot up. I had an alibi. I didn't have to act like this was an accident to protect myself. I didn't have to make him disappear and try to cover my crime.

"Of course," I breathed out.

Accidents happened. They were tragic, but they weren't a missing or murdered body. Lucy could have gotten over an accident, and me...I would have caught everything on my camera. Filming used to mean everything to me. Documentation served as trophies. *Proof.* The realest horror movie one could ever make. And I had tapes, all kinds, just like the one Lucy caught me watching. Ones that mattered nothing to me now. Ones I would get rid of the moment this was over. *The men.*

"What? What...did you remember?"

I glanced to Jeff, but reached forward, picking up a large rock. "I remembered a stupid boy who was greedy for the wrong thing. A boy who was more focused on reliving deaths, he lost sight of why he wanted to commit them to begin with. I remember a coward who didn't go after what he wanted—Lucy. You killed him, though. Thank you for that. But now it's time I finish what he started."

"No. No!" Jeff tried to buck me off. I was lighter now, but I still had the upper-hand. Slamming my fist down, a loud smack cracked through the air. Blood sprayed, gushing from the seams of the crater centered in his forehead. Jeff's arms slowed, and his eyes rolled. I lifted to strike again, seeing where he'd hit Lucy with the flashlight while they were searching for the cabin. It flashed so fast, sending my arm to the side as I came in at a side angle. The rock was so big, it barely fit in my hand. Pieces broke off as the bone over his eyebrow caved in. Crimson seeped and pooled at the innermost cover of his eye. I wasn't done, but I forced myself to stop as Dr. Patron's words crept in. *"Lucy's almost yours. I've taught you what you need to know, and you've come far. But you must control what's inside when the time comes. If you can do that and follow my rules, you've won."*

I dropped the rock, moving back to rest against the tree a foot away. Labored breaths left Jeff. Gurgling sounds as he fought to live. Each short gasp was a relief symbolizing a true beginning. A new life without obstacles. An evil smile came to my face. Moments dragged out. His fingers twitched, straightening and shaking as his muscles flexed through the fight. Then, nothing. There was no need for words as I watched his one good eye bulge, then go lax. Death had him, and the fear cementing his face reflected the fact. It was sweeter than anything thus far. *Lucy.* I had her all to myself now. She was all I had ever wanted. All that mattered. Our always had arrived with his departure. Our forever…it was just beginning.

****

Memories came. A flash here and there. Intense colors. Warping walls of pictures that stole me away from Lucy. I cared for none of them. I didn't need them now that we'd started our new life.

Jeff's death hit her hard, but it wasn't something I couldn't bring her back from. More patience. More wooing and building her up. School approached and passed. I didn't go back. The city held secrets—ones I didn't believe would come out—but I took absolutely zero risks concerning her.

My evidence of past therapy sessions, my old films of torturing and killing the men, everything connected to the old me lay in ashes in the fireplace. There was nothing she would run across, nothing that tied me to any crime whatsoever. It was all water under the bridge, and what we had was deeper than any depth of love imaginable.

For the first time in my life, I was truly happy. *She was happy.*

As we boxed up the last of our things from the guesthouse, I stole glances at her. A soft tune hummed through our space and blonde hair fell over her shoulder as she folded a shirt, placing it in the overnight bag we were taking for the trip. The move to Florida was easy enough to decide. I got accepted there for my new school—a degree in Business, and she was starting prerequisites for nursing. We already had a place to live, and Dr. Patron's summer house was only a few blocks away from our beach cottage. I didn't think I needed to continue the sessions, but in the last few weeks, I came to see how vital it was for me to confess my sins—confess the obsession that still festered when I didn't feel I could ever get enough of her. It calmed the beast within—the one who carefully watched *every look, every move*, made by *anyone* who got too close to her.

Lucy grabbed a sundress, pausing as she caught my movement. The smile that came had the heaviness she caused inside to thicken. My heart rate accelerated, and I left the box I'd meant to carry down to our new SUV.

I walked slow…methodical, taking a wide path around the sofa. Her head jerked to the side and her lids narrowed playfully. She shot across the bed, racing for the door, but she wasn't fast enough. A squeal left her as my arms wrapped around her waist and I spun her back to the bed, bending to flatten her against the mattress with my weight. Her ass moved against my cock while she tried to wiggle free. The pleasure sent a growl leaving me as I bit into her neck.

"Was this morning not enough? We're never going to get on the road if this continues."

I sucked against her skin, already jerking at the button of her jeans and shoving her pants down. My tongue flattened, licking so I could taste her. For the briefest moment, I was better than okay. I was thriving in everything she was.

"Boston," Lucy moaned, reaching back to place her palm on the side of my forehead right over my scar. I fit myself against her entrance, easing the head inside. "Wait. Not yet. You have to say it first."

My lips traveled to her ear and I moaned as I surged forward. "I love you. I fucking love you. All day. Every day. Always."

A cry sounded out as fingers gripped into my hair. The sting from her pull registered, but got stolen through the frenzy that erupted as her pussy pulsed around me.

In the blur of hard thrusts, everything tuned out. Everything but the wetness and tone of her voice as she mumbled my name. Her smell engulfed me, feeding my speed. Thoughts were pointless when I had everything I ever needed before me.

My hips slapped into her ass, and she arched just like I loved. The action spoke of her desires. It showed how much she needed me too. When I was buried deep inside her pussy, it ruled everything for both of us. It was the only time we could be one.

More moans. More sighs. I swallowed them whole as my lips massaged into hers. The suction on my tongue had my hand wrapping around her throat. My cock swelled, thickening. Lucy's body jolted in spasms, and I groaned, not holding back. My cum shot deep. Me—in her. The calm. The sating sensation that put me at peace. Her heart and life beat against my fingertips from her pulse point, and it was the most beautiful rhythm in the world. For seconds, I didn't move. I didn't want the moment to ever end. Because of my love, now they never would.

The End

Thank you for reading!
Share your thoughts and reactions with a review!

About the Author

Alaska Angelini is a Best Selling Author of dark, twisted happily-ever-afters. She currently resides in Wisconsin, but moves at the drop of a dime. Check back in a few months and she's guaranteed to live somewhere new.

Obsessive, stalking, mega-alpha hero's/anti-heros are her thing. Throw in some rope, cuffs, and a whip or two, and watch the magic begin.

If you're looking to connect with her to learn more, feel free to email her at alaska_angelini@yahoo.com, or find her on Facebook. You can also stop by her website http://www.alaskaangelini.com.

Twitter: http://twitter.com/alaskaangelini
Goodreads: http://goodreads.com/alaskaangelini
Pinterest: http://pinterest.com/alaskaangelini
Newletter: http://alaskaangelini.us9.list-manage1.com/subscribe?u=bab41358f98da39a35c46dccb&id=19172fa88c

Other titles from this Author:

A. A. Dark
Mad Girl (The Chronicles of Anna Monroe)
24690
White Out (24690-Book 2)
27001 (Welcome to Whitlock #1)

Alaska Angelini
Unbearable
SLADE: Captive to the Dark
BLAKE: Captive to the Dark
GAIGE: Captive to the Dark
LILY: Captive to the Dark, Special Edition 1
CHASE: Dark and Dangerous CCTD Set 2
Watch Me: Stalked
Rush
Dom Up: Devlin Black 1
Dom Fever: Devlin Black 2
This Dom: Devlin Black 3

Dark Paranormal lover? Check out Alaska's other reads ...

Wolf (Wolf River 1) *Optioned for FILM!
Prey: Marko Delacroix 1
Blood Bound: Marko Delacroix 2
Lure: Marko Delacroix 3
Rule: Marko Delacroix 4
Reign: Marko Delacroix 5

COMING SOON!

The Chronicles of Anna Monroe

MASTER MIND

An Anna Monroe and Never Far crossover.

BEST SELLING AUTHOR ALASKA ANGELINI WRITING AS

A. A. Dark

Also Coming Soon!

27009

WELCOME TO WHITLOCK
Book 2

A. A. Dark

Printed in Great Britain
by Amazon

If you want to increase your success rate,

DOUBLE your failure rate.

~ Thomas J. Watson